She had...

He found it ~~hard to~~ believe Sara had a teenage son—their son. Why hadn't she tried to contact him? He silently admitted there wasn't an iron-clad guarantee that the boy was his, but he remembered the old Sara, and he couldn't imagine she would have gone from him to someone else. What they had shared had been too special for her to dismiss him so casually. Although, Jess reminded himself, she had left without a word to him . . .

Her wrists were so tiny he could have circled them with his fingers, her throat equally delicate. He had always been so careful with her, afraid he would hurt her, but all she ever told him was that she loved everything that had to do with him. So, if she loved him that much, why did she leave without a word? Why had she run away?

Dear Reader:

We at Silhouette are very excited to bring you a NEW reading **Sensation**. *Look out for the four books which will appear in our new Silhouette* **Sensation** *series every month. These stories will have the high quality you have come to expect from Silhouette, and their varied and provocative plots will encourage you to explore the wonder of falling in love – again and again!*

Emotions run high in these drama-filled novels. Greater sensual detail and an extra edge of realism intensify the hero and heroine's relationship so that you cannot help but be caught up in their every change of mood.

We hope you enjoy this new **Sensation** – *and will go on to enjoy many more.*

We would love to hear your comments about our new line and encourage you to write to us:

Jane Nicholls
Silhouette Books
PO Box 236
Thornton Road
Croydon
Surrey
CR9 3RU

LINDA RANDALL WISDOM
We Give Thanks

Silhouette Sensation

First published in Great Britain in 1989
by Silhouette Books, Eton House, 18–24 Paradise Road,
Richmond, Surrey TW9 1SR

© Linda Randall Wisdom 1988

Silhouette, Silhouette Sensation and Colophon are
Trade Marks of Harlequin Enterprises B.V.

ISBN 0 373 57578 5

18–8906

Made and printed in Great Britain

Chapter One

"Hey, don't I get some service around here?"

Sara straightened up, her hand rubbing her lower back, sore from bending over a car's fender for the past hour. She peered out of the darkened interior of the garage toward the gas pumps, hoping her ears had lied to her. No, that was Albert all right. She walked slowly out to the pumps under the bright gaze of a thirty-five-year-old man going on ten. She knew from experience what he was like when he was in his macho-man role, acting like the town stud. Town dud was more like it, she scoffed. His eyes were already stripping her faded jeans and cotton shirt away from her body, and she had barely gone five steps.

"Damn, Sara, you're sure lookin' good today," he told her, leaning back against the hood of his pickup, his brawny arms crossed in front of his chest, just above the beer belly hanging over the waistband of his worn jeans. "Good enough to eat."

"I'd give you heartburn," she said caustically, unscrewing the gas cap. She poked the nozzle into the tank and stuck the cap under the nozzle grip so it would pump unattended.

"Say, darlin', it's too nice a day for you to be cooped up here. I'm driving into Charlotte. Why don't you come with me?" he coaxed. "We could even stop somewhere on the way back for an hour or two of privacy."

"Why don't you ask your wife to go with you? I can imagine she doesn't get out much what with looking after all those kids." Sara hated herself for sounding so waspish when she wanted to sound cold, but she hated the men who undressed her with their eyes and muttered their lewd comments. She hated it all.

Albert was undaunted. He watched Sara withdraw the nozzle from the tank.

"Lookin' at you sure makes the day brighter, pretty Sara." He pressed the money in her hand, his fingers rubbing her arm in a not too soothing caress. "Maybe I should've had you check the oil. I sure do like watching the way your pretty little rear moves when you're hanging over my fender." He smiled broadly.

She stepped back, her eloquent eyes speaking what her lips refused to.

Albert laughed heartily and climbed into the truck. He tipped his billed cap to her in a mocking salute and drove off in a cloud of dust.

Sara returned to the garage to finish the oil change she was working on before she had been so rudely interrupted. On her way she stopped in the rest room. Staring into the speckled mirror, she saw silvery blond hair escaping the braid she had fixed that morning and her face shiny from lack of makeup. Not a very glamorous picture. She sighed, turning away.

She suddenly visualized herself dressed like someone out of a fashion magazine. Her hair would be caught up in a fancy twist, and she would wear a pretty dress and have makeup on her face. Oh, yes, she would look and feel pretty, and she wouldn't find one pair of worn jeans or grubby shirts in her closet. And her nails wouldn't always have grease under them and— She shook her head almost violently to stem the flow of tears that was sure to come next. Sara had gone this long without feeling sorry for herself. This wasn't the time to start. After all, she had an oil change to finish, and by then Jackson should be back with that special order of spare parts.

An hour later the oil change was finished, and Jackson still wasn't back. Sara began to feel apprehensive. Where was he?

"Afternoon, Sara." A silver-haired man in his seventies walked slowly up the drive.

"Reverend, you shouldn't have walked up here in this heat," she scolded, ushering him into the office. "I told you I'd deliver your car to you."

"You're sounding just like Mrs. Harris," he said testily, taking the chair she offered and lowering his bony frame into it. "I may have one foot in the grave, but that doesn't mean the other is standing on a banana peel just yet."

Sara worked hard to hide her smile. Reverend Mapes enjoyed sounding like a crotchety old man, but she knew all too well what a kindhearted person he truly was. He had been the pastor of the church she had attended ever since she could remember, and he had married her parents in the small, white frame church several blocks away. She would miss him.

"Reverend, what will I do without you?" she whispered, grasping his hand tightly, feeling the fragile bones beneath her fingertips.

He smiled. "You'll do fine, Sara. You're a very strong woman. You've had to be all these years." His faded brown eyes watched her behind his wire-rimmed spectacles. He understood her worries, and he wanted to reassure her that he had put her in good hands, but he couldn't assure her about something that he didn't feel certain about. He was leaving the area due to poor health that required a drier climate, and a new minister would soon take over his duties.

Sara roused herself quickly and released his hand. "If I'm not more careful, one of the good ladies from the Home Mission Society might come along and say I'm corrupting you," she said with a brittle laugh.

He shook his head, looking too somber for her peace of mind. Reverend Mapes knew only too well the trials Sara had endured in the small town. Even in the eighties an unwed mother did not go unnoticed, and when she owned a business the townspeople needed, well, that just made matters worse. How the tongues wagged the day old man Carson's will was read disclosing he had left everything to Sara.

"Always knew she was up to no good when she moved in with that old man," one woman sniffed.

"She turned his head, that's what she did."

"Humph! An old man and her so young. It's easy to guess what she did to get put in his will."

Sara's thoughts echoed the reverend's. Funny how a woman could live all her life in the same town, except for a couple of years away at college, and it only took those two years to change her life, not to mention her reputation. Funny and very sad.

"In high school I used to be called Sara the Saint, because I wouldn't go out to the pond alone with a boy," she mused bitterly. "Now I'm called Sara the Slut. It doesn't take much, does it?"

Reverend Mapes shook his head. It was a shame someone so young should be so bitter, and he told her so as he rose slowly to his feet. "I better be heading home before Mrs. Harris sends out a posse." He smiled, reaching into his pocket and withdrawing a worn leather wallet. "How much do I owe you?"

She shook her head and stood back. "Reverend, have I ever charged you for such minor work before?" she chided, a ghost of a smile touching her lips.

"None of your work is minor," he retorted, slipping his wallet back into his pocket. He knew from past experience that Sara refused any money from him for small repairs on his car, and the one time he had insisted she take the money he had watched her the following Sunday, with a broad smile on her face, drop that same money in the collection plate. "You don't make any money this way, Sara. I know you haven't charged Mrs. Gold a fraction of what she really owes for her gas for the last two years."

She flushed. "She lost a great deal of her savings when she was conned by that so-called bonds salesman," she muttered. "Besides, that old clunker of hers doesn't take all that much gas anyway, and at least it takes regular."

Reverend Mapes chuckled. "You're a wonderful woman, Sara. I'll miss you."

Her smile wobbled. "I'll miss you, too. Do me a favor, will you? Ask the new pastor not to run me out of town too soon. I want to make sure to have everything packed first."

"Oh, ye of little faith," he intoned, walking outside to his car and getting inside. "I'll see you on Sunday,

Sara. Don't be late. The new minister will be there, and I don't want him to have a bad first impression of you."

She laughed and waved him off. She had turned around to reenter the office when a wheezing pickup pulled up to the garage opening.

"It's about time you got back, Jackson," she said to the old man climbing out of the cab. "Where have you been?" He didn't bother answering, because he was too busy swearing at the truck, which emitted a cloud of steam from under the hood.

"Damn truck ain't good for much 'cept for collectin' rust," he grumbled, kicking one of the tires.

"If you'd take a little extra time and work on it, you wouldn't be threatening to put it out to pasture every five minutes," Sara told him, looking into the truck bed to make sure he had gotten everything she needed. She'd bet he had a brown paper bag in the cab holding the whiskey he drank—for medicinal purposes, he explained. He believed the fiery alcohol was better than any multivitamin manufactured. Since he hadn't been sick in more than thirty years, people had to wonder how right he was. Jackson peered into the garage.

"You take the car over to the reverend?" he asked in a voice made rough from the cigars he smoked.

"He walked over to pick it up." She began unloading the truck and carrying the packages into the garage. "Come on, help me with these. They're heavy."

Jackson grumbled loud and strong the entire time they unloaded the truck, but Sara didn't care as long as he did his share. She smiled as she listened to him mumbling to himself. She saw his grumbling as part of his charm. Sara couldn't remember a time when he hadn't been around. He had been a close friend of Harvey's, and he never said a word against her when

Harvey had taken a teary-eyed, pregnant Sara into his home, cared for her during the last months of her pregnancy, driven her to the hospital when her baby was born and left her the gas station in his will along with enough money to Jackson to keep him from feeling dependent on anyone. When Sara had once asked him if he resented Harvey not leaving the station to him, he had loudly protested, "Hell, no! That would mean I'd have to do real work when now I just work when I feel like it. 'Sides, he knew you'd need some security for that kid of yours." She had smiled at that. Jackson's favorite name for all men was bastard, another part of his homegrown charm, but he had never called Tim that. Even when the now fifteen-year-old boy deserved it, which was more often than she cared to think about.

"I thought Tim was coming by after school to help you," he rumbled, putting away the boxes of oil and filters.

"He was." Her clipped tone was answer enough. How many other times had her son promised to do something for her and hadn't come through? About as many times as Sara wished she had moved somewhere else, where Tim might have been able to live a more normal life. Had she been wrong in staying here? Would both of them, especially Tim, have been better off in a town where no one knew of her past? She could always have posed as a widow or a divorcée.

"You wanna get your brain back where it belongs?" Jackson's raspy voice intruded into her thoughts. "We gotta lot of work to do here before dinner."

Sara looked up, then flushed when she realized she had probably been standing there holding the boxes for the last few minutes.

"If a woman wants to daydream, she can," she retorted with a touch of the asperity she used to be known for. "Besides, *you* should talk when it comes to work."

Jackson grinned as he turned away.

"Let's get this stuff put away and close up the garage," Sara said, heading back out to the truck. They kept the gas pumps open until eight, since the house was behind the gas station and they could hear incoming customers from there, thanks to Harvey's foresight in installing a buzzer wired into the kitchen.

"What we havin' for dinner?"

"Beef stew," she replied, going into the office and picking up the day's receipts.

"With dumplings?"

Sara smiled, well aware Jackson didn't consider stew complete without fluffy dumplings. "Would I fix stew without dumplings?"

A half hour later she was in the kitchen cutting up fresh vegetables for a salad. Jackson would remain at the gas station until dinnertime.

Sara knew why she was feeling sorry for herself. This was the month it had all begun. More than sixteen years ago she had been working part-time as a waitress in a coffee shop while going to school, and one evening a young man had come into the restaurant and sat down at one of her tables. A young man who changed her life and broke her heart. Even if she had wanted to forget him, she couldn't. Not when her son had his eyes and smile. She didn't regret having Tim, and while her hometown hadn't exactly welcomed her back with open arms, she still hadn't regretted one thing she had done over the years. She just wished Tim wasn't so bitter.

"Hey." The object of her thoughts breezed through the back door and filched a slice of carrot. "When's dinner?"

Sara stopped her work and turned to face him. Long, shaggy hair the same dark brown as his eyes, a face that would be handsome if he didn't look so sullen most of the time and a mouth that usually looked angry. He was taller than she was, his height another legacy from his father.

"I thought you were going to come by the station to help out when you got out of school," she reproached him. "We had a lot of parts to put away, and we could have used you."

He shrugged. "I forgot." He pulled off a ragged denim jacket to reveal an equally ragged T-shirt.

"You went to school looking like that?" Sara practically wailed. "Tim, you look like a bum."

"Teachers believe I'm one anyway. Why not make it easy for them?" He tried to snatch a cucumber slice, but her slapping hand stopped him until his hand snaked around hers and stole it anyway. He flashed her a broad grin as his white teeth bit into the slice.

Sara's eyes narrowed. "You didn't go to school today, did you?" She sighed. She knew the truth from his silence.

Tim saw the sorrow on his mother's face and instantly melted. Whatever else he was—and his teachers had quite a few names for him—he did love his mother, and he wouldn't do anything to intentionally hurt her. But how could he explain that he didn't care for school and didn't see where it would get him? Oh, sure, he knew what the counselors said about his having a high IQ and how he had the potential to do great things if he would just get off his butt and apply himself. Apply himself, hell, all he wanted to do was get a job, make good money and get his mom out of this stinking town. He wanted to see her smile more and look happy all the time. That he just might be a good part of her worries hadn't even occurred to him.

"Dinner will be ready soon. Would you please call Jackson and then wash up?" Sara asked, carrying the salad bowl over to the table.

Tim opened the back door and leaned out. "Jackson, dinner's ready!" he shouted and closed the door again.

Sara stared at him as he washed up at the sink. "I believe I asked you to *call* him, not shout the windows out."

Tim tore off a paper towel and dried his hands. "You know he can't hear a damn thing without the hearing aid he refuses to wear half the time."

Sara wanted to laugh at the frustration bubbling up inside her. She had reprimanded Tim in the past for swearing, but she was positive he said much worse when she wasn't around her, so she tried to ignore his color-ful language more often than not in hopes he'd soon realize profanity didn't make the world any better. She rarely swore, basically because she didn't like the sound of it. So when she tripped over the coffee table and broke her little toe, Tim had scolded her for using bad language, then assisted her into the car and driven her to the emergency clinic, all the time ignoring her alarmed protests that he didn't have a driver's license yet, much less a permit. Like his father, rules never oc-curred to Tim. Perhaps that was why Sara loved him so much, teenage rebellions and all.

During dinner Sara looked over her companions, lis-tening to a repeat of many other dinnertime conversations. Jackson railed at Tim for not helping his mother and always raising hell when he should be working harder in school so he could make something of himself. Tim countered with the argument that there was nothing to make when there were so few jobs around, except for the textile mill outside of town, and he wanted more for his life than working as a mill hand. The arguments, which never grew heated, were so familiar to Sara that she tended to tune them out.

Tim looked at the unseeing glaze in his mother's eyes and knew what caused it. After seeing it this time every year, he soon figured out it had something to do with his father. His heart hardened against the man who had given him life, and he daily cursed him for leaving Sara when she had needed him most. The fact that there had been many times Tim had needed him never came up, because he had convinced himself a long time ago that he didn't need anyone. But he vowed to always be there for his mother; he knew she had no one else to count on, except for Jackson. Tim brushed a wayward strand of hair away from his face and concentrated on his second helping of stew.

Later, when Sara stood up to gather the plates for washing, Tim stopped her.

"I'll do them," he offered roughly, jumping to his feet and taking the dishes out of her hands.

Sara smiled. She knew this was his way of apologizing for not being at the station that afternoon. She would probably end up with a broken glass or plate, if not both, but it was worth it.

"Then, if no one would mind, I think I'll go upstairs and soak in a hot tub," she said brightly.

"Those long baths addle the brain!" Jackson shouted after her as she left the kitchen.

"That's something you couldn't know about since you only believe in baths on Saturday nights," Tim retorted with a rare teasing grin.

"Boy, you gonna talk like that, I just might not stay here and help you with all those dishes," Jackson threw back.

"That kind of help I don't need!"

A lively argument followed Sara into her bathroom. She laughed as she pinned her hair on top of her head and turned on the faucets full blast.

When she was luxuriating in the hot frothy water, she realized she couldn't hear anything coming from the kitchen and idly wondered why the two men had lowered their voices. She had a sneaking suspicion that they were speaking softly because she was the object of their conversation and promptly decided to lengthen their list of household chores the next day. She hated the idea that they had so much time on their hands they could stand around talking instead of working.

"IT ISN'T RIGHT she has to put up with that kind of crap around here," Tim said, washing a glass with more force than necessary. "If she was smart, she'd sell the station and go someplace where she could have a normal life. She's talked about it before, but for some reason she won't do it."

"And do what if she did move away? Your ma never finished gettin' her degree. She don't have no skills but what Harvey and me taught her," Jackson argued. "You tell me how many gas stations would hire a woman to do the work she does here, not to mention pay her enough money to support the two of you."

"Then I'll get a job and support her."

"Ha! That's a dumb idea and you know it. What can you do 'sides hot-wire a car?" Jackson scorned. "All that'll get you is a few years in a detention home, and you wouldn't be much help to her there, would you?"

Tim flushed, a sure sign of the anger he felt at himself more than at the man who was honestly trying to help him. He hated being young and he hated this town. While many people looked for the peace and solitude Henderson, North Carolina offered, he wasn't one of them. He knew the constant fights he got into at school upset his mother and likewise upset him, because he loved her dearly. The trouble was, she didn't know what was said and had been said over the years, because he didn't want her to know. From the first time he had been called a bastard, he had fought back the only way he knew how—with his fists. By now he didn't know any other way. While many boys his age were caught up in sports and girls, he rode his motorcycle all over the countryside, looking for a place where no one cared about his parentage. He just couldn't understand what his mother saw in this town. Ever since he could remember, most of the people here treated her like dirt, and she took it quietly. And she wasn't a wimp; no, he knew better. But every time he talked to her about moving, she only shook her head and talked about roots.

Roots. That seemed a funny word to come from someone whose parents couldn't handle her pregnancy and didn't know what to do or say to her and who, in the end, allowed her to move out, because she couldn't handle their silent looks of reproach and her mother's continual talk of ruining her life. Tim learned more about his grandparents from Jackson than from his mother and was relieved they had died years ago when he was still a young boy. All Sara ever said about her parents was that they had been unhappy people and should be viewed as such. Tim was glad he had never known them, since they had refused to have anything to do with their grandson. He'd seen them at a distance many times, but they never acknowledged him, and in his anger at their treatment of his mother, he wouldn't have wanted anything to do with them anyway. Instead, he went on loving his mother in the best way he knew how. Deep down he was aware it was the wrong way, because he also hurt her, but what else could he do? It was at times like this he wished he had someone to talk to. To find out why he felt the way he did. Then maybe he wouldn't hurt so much inside.

At the same time would he really want to move away now, when the most beautiful girl he had ever seen had just moved into town and attended his school? Lora Summers had mink-brown hair, hazel eyes and the prettiest smile, and since her first day at school Tim hadn't missed his English class once so he could sit across from her and just look. So far he hadn't felt comfortable enough to say even one word to her.

Amazingly Tim finished the dishes without a single mishap, considering his thoughts weren't once on his task. He tossed the towel into the sink and turned to Jackson, who sat at the table with his glass of whiskey.

"It's all his fault," Tim told him. There was no need to identify who. Tim's fury at the man who had fathered him had grown throughout the years. "If he showed up now, I'd shoot him dead."

Jackson shook his head. "No, boy, that wouldn't get you nothing but more misery. From what Sara once said, he never knew where she came from. When she tried to contact him through his parents, she was told they didn't know or care where he was. I want to see the girl happy again, and I wish she would have married."

Tim wasn't sure he liked that idea, because he would have had to share his mother with someone else, and who was to say another man would want him around. In fact, he had an idea one or two of the men who wanted to marry her years ago didn't want a ready-made family. He picked up his jacket and shrugged it on.

"You shouldn't be going out on a school night," Jackson said, watching him open the door.

"No, but that's never stopped me before." He slammed the door behind him. The roar of his motor-cycle was heard next.

Jackson slowly rose to his feet and walked out to the living room to watch television.

"Sara, *Dynasty*'s on," he shouted. "You gonna come out and watch it?"

"I don't think so," she called back. "Is Tim out there with you?"

"No, he left a few minutes ago."

There was only a long charged silence after his reply. Jackson wished he hadn't had to tell her and damned the boy for making life so difficult for her.

When Sara emerged from her bath a half hour later, she found Jackson snoozing in the easy chair in front of the television and Tim gone. She poured herself a glass of wine and curled up on the couch to watch TV. She knew it wouldn't be long before Jackson woke up, loudly insisting he hadn't fallen asleep, that he was just resting his eyes. Sara would smile and agree, and before too long she would go to bed to lie awake until Tim came home. She wanted to tell her son she feared these nights. She wanted to beg him to talk to her, to tell her what he was feeling inside, and that if they could talk it all out, just maybe he wouldn't feel so angry at the world. She began to wish he was five years old again. Things were so much simpler then.

WHEN SARA ARRIVED the next morning, Jackson was already there at the station sitting in a chair just outside the office, sipping a cup of coffee and watching cars head out of town toward the mill. Sara poured herself a cup and sipped carefully, knowing Jackson's coffee tended to be a little water mixed in with the grounds. As usual it was strong enough to float the entire U.S. Navy. She glanced at the dusty, dark blue pickup waiting inside the garage. "Is that Calvin's truck?" she groaned.

"Yep. He claims it needs a tune-up," Jackson told her.

Sara grimaced and glanced around warily. "Where is he? Generally he insists on remaining the entire time complaining how we charge too much and we're too slow. Then he'll threaten to take his truck to Charlotte next time. I don't know if he's worth all the trouble."

"Said he wanted to walk over to Hank's for a haircut. He may complain but he always pays in cash," he reminded her.

"I guess he's worth the trouble."

The day turned out to be slow. Jackson tuned up the truck, and as Sara predicted, the owner, one of Jackson's poker-playing cronies, stayed to watch and tell Jackson how to do his work. Sara remained in the office working on the books, only stopping when someone pulled up for gas.

When a dark blue Toyota sedan stopped, Sara's face lit up, and she hurried out to the pumps.

"Hello, Sara." A sprightly redhead hopped out of the car. "How is it going?"

"Same as always. How are you doing, Tess?" Sara opened the gas cap and pushed in the nozzle.

"I'd be fine if I had more hours in the day," she replied. "It seems everyone needs Mom to go to the cleaners or to pick up the shoes at the repair shop or buy milk, and so what if she has plans of her own. Moms are superwomen and can get everything done with ease." Tess took in her friend's pale features and the evidence of a sleepless night in her eyes. "Why don't you go shopping with me?" she suggested. "We could have a day to ourselves, eat something fattening for lunch and all that good stuff."

"No, thanks, Tess. I have so much to do around here," Sara said a bit too cheerfully.

Tess shook her head. "You've never been a very good liar, Sara Murdock. Even when we were eight and you told Mr. Samuels you broke his window when Cal was the one who did it, Mr. Samuels could tell you were lying. Your face always gets that funny shade of pink, and you can never look anyone in the eye. And don't give me your scarlet-woman routine either. You need to get out more. Living here with a teenage son and an old man isn't good for you. When was the last time you had a day all to yourself? Come to think of it, when was the last time you had a date?"

Sara smiled. "The last time I attended a church social, Mrs. Masterson almost had a coronary."

"Big deal! She has one every week like clockwork," Tess scoffed. "Besides, church functions don't count. You need to go out with a man and do something totally frivolous."

"Tess, in case you haven't noticed, there isn't exactly an influx of single men in this town," Sara pointed out.

"All right, play stubborn. You've always been good at that. You will be at church Sunday, though, to see the new minister, won't you? Mrs. Harris said he's a very well-mannered young man and should be a contribution to the community." She imitated the minister's housekeeper's nasal tones. "Of course, sixty could be young to her."

"Have I ever missed church? You know how much Mrs. Masterson enjoys seeing me there and telling me how she's praying for my soul."

Sara's lighthearted tone was a sham, and Tess knew it. She also knew she was one of the few to stand behind her friend during her trouble and was grateful her husband refused to listen to some of the other men's ribald comments regarding Sara's morals. Instead, Charlie told them what they could do with their ideas. Tess had sat with Sara on many nights when she felt sorry for herself and wished she had remained in Henderson instead of going away to school. The only thing Sara refused to share with Tess, or anyone, was the man's name. For all these years Sara never mentioned the man she had fallen in love with and conceived a child with. Tess hurt for her friend and would do anything for her. Right now she wanted to see her happy, and her idea of happy was to have a loving man by her side. But Sara was right, there weren't that many eligible men in town.

Tess glanced over at the pump to see the amount owed and dug into her purse for her wallet. "Are you sure you won't go shopping with me? We haven't had a day out together in ages."

"No, thanks, I have too much to do here."

"Then will you promise to think about taking a day off in the next week or so?"

"If I can," was all Sara would say. Tess bluntly told her she didn't believe one word she said, but her tone carried the affection of a longtime friendship. Sara remained by the pumps and watched her friend drive away with a honk of the horn and a wave. Tess had been wonderful to her over the years, and she only wished she could do more in return.

"WE'RE GOING TO ROAST in that old building," Tim muttered, as they left the car and walked toward the large, white, painted clapboard church Sara had attended since childhood.

"You haven't yet, so I wouldn't worry about it now. Miss Lawrence, how are you?" Sara smiled at a silver-haired woman who walked slowly ahead of them. The woman had been her first-grade teacher and was known to never forget a pupil in the many years she had taught school.

"Good morning, Sara. I am doing well, and you certainly look cool and refreshing today in that blue dress." The merciless dark eyes stared at Tim, who shifted uneasily under her regard. "Timothy, I do hope you've given up some of your bad habits."

"Miss Lawrence," he muttered.

"That was one of them right there," the retired teacher rapped out in a voice still strong. "You never spoke up. You must learn to speak clearly, my boy."

"Yes'm."

Sara shifted her eyes toward her son as the elderly woman walked ahead of them. "She never forgets any of her past students."

"No kidding. I just wish I was one she would forget. Jackson's smart to stay home," he mumbled, as they walked up the dusty path to the church.

"Jackson just likes to brag to everyone he's a heathen," she replied, waving to one woman who had called out her name. "He hasn't attended church in more than thirty years, and I think he's afraid to break his perfect record."

Sara doubted anything had changed in the fifteen years she had come with Tim in tow, from the time he was a tiny baby to now. Quite a few people, generally those in her age group, greeted her with natural smiles and questions about her health. She realized the people who viewed her more dimly were members of another age, who would brand any unwed mother with colorful morals without bothering to look into the circumstances or even care that the woman was a longtime member of their town and hadn't done anything wrong, other than to have her child alone. After living with Jackson for so long she knew better than most that old habits were hard to break, especially among the older people. They were the ones who nodded coolly, if acknowledging her at all, and walked on into the foyer. Among these "upright" citizens Tim stayed close to his mother and scowled at the gray-haired and blue-rinsed ladies, his swaggering stance giving credibility to their predictions that "nothing good will come from that boy, just wait and see."

Sara nodded politely to Mrs. Masterson, a plump woman in her sixties who hadn't had a kind word for anyone in more than forty years. She didn't notice Tim offer a shy smile to the young girl following Mrs. Masterson, but the older woman had and immediately ushered her granddaughter inside. As one of the leading matriarchs in Henderson's limited society no one dared openly defy her, except for Sara. She knew every time she walked into the same room the older woman was in, she defied her, and while Sara never gloated or treated her with the least bit of disrespect, Mrs. Masterson still viewed her as an undesirable. Sara doubted that the woman's opinion of her would ever change.

"Have you seen the new minister yet?" Carol Peterson, another old friend since grade school, edged up behind Sara.

"No, why?"

"Sara, if I wasn't married, I'd be inviting that man over for Sunday dinner every week." She wrinkled her nose in delight. "He is positively yummy. And single to boot."

She chuckled. "That good, huh?" She glanced toward the front, but could only see Reverend Mapes's kindly features as he talked to another man, tall and dark haired. For a moment she felt something tickle the back of her memory, but just as quickly she squelched it. No, the last place she would see him would be here. Jess wasn't the churchgoing type. Funny how she would think of him after so long. Maybe Tess was right, and she should consider dating again. Too bad the only new single man in town was the minister. She smothered a laugh. That would certainly set a few people back on their ears if she caught the man's eye.

"Good? I'll be having a rough time listening to any sermon, because I'll be too busy looking at him," Carol said. "You know, with him so dark and you so blond, you'd make a good-looking couple."

Sara glanced in Mrs. Masterson's direction. "I'm sure that would really set a few people back," she said drily. "They'd probably order me burned at the stake for seducing a man of God. No, I think I'd be better off doing my looking out of town."

Carol groaned as she heard a loudly voiced "Mom!"

"They're probably arguing over who sits closest to the aisle." She referred to her seven-year-old twin sons. "See you later."

When the organ began to play the opening music, Sara walked down the aisle toward the pew she usually sat in. This was one of the times she enjoyed best, listening to the soft strains of the opening hymn and allowing her mind to clear of everything but the hour ahead. She glanced through the bulletin to read the many announcements. She noted she was scheduled to work in the nursery next week and dug into her purse for a pen to circle the date. She glanced up, smiling at the warm features of Reverend Mapes, then her smile froze when her eyes shifted to the younger man seated beside him. The man she had only seen from the back a few moments ago. A man with chestnut-colored hair and deep brown eyes, a man whose smile likewise stilled when his gaze alighted on her and his eyes widened in recognition.

"No," she whispered hoarsely, fighting the white spots dancing before her eyes. "No." Memories flooded back with a vengeance. Times of laughter, of loving, of tears. Times she had forgotten over the years, because she had no choice but to do so and because a young woman's love for a young man couldn't survive as she matured. "No, it's all a dream. A very bad dream."

"Mom?" Tim looked at her, his face pale with alarm as he watched her stunned expression turn to horror. "Mom, what's wrong?"

She wanted to laugh. Carol said he was yummy. Yes, she had once thought that. Sara sat there waiting for hurt and anger to wash over her, but nothing happened. It was all gone as it should be. Sometimes in the dead of night she wondered what would happen if she saw him again. Now she knew, and she still thought about laughing, but she was afraid if she started she wouldn't be able to stop. Lost in the dark gray haze surrounding her, she didn't realize the man she had stared at so intently had half risen from his seat, because she had already sunk into a deep, dark sea of forgetfulness. Just as the darkness overtook her she wondered if everything would be back to normal when she woke up and the man up there would turn out to be anyone but Jess.

Chapter Two

"What do you think caused it?" one voice asked.

"You don't think she could be well . . . well, *that* way again, do you? After all, if it happened once there's no reason why it couldn't happen again." Only Mrs. Masterson would ask such a crass question, Sara told herself while floating in the warm, comfortable world she presently resided in. She had no desire to leave. She felt the sensation of lying on something not very comfortable, but she still wasn't about to leave her safe little world. She probably would have laughed at Mrs. Masterson's assumption if she had had the energy. Somehow the idea of her being pregnant again sounded very funny when she couldn't even remember the last time she'd had a date.

"Perhaps if you would give her some air, she could recover sooner," Tess said, exasperated with the nosy women.

There were a few murmurs of protest and unwanted advice before Tess finally spoke to Sara in her no-nonsense voice, "All right, Sara, come back to earth. Everyone is gone now, and I have a few questions for you."

Sara slowly opened her eyes and took in her surroundings. She knew she must be in the small room off to the side of the sanctuary that was usually used for the brides to wait in. How inappropriate for her to be here, she thought almost hysterically.

"Why did you faint?" Tess asked bluntly.

Sara struggled to sit up on the small couch. "I must be coming down with something," she said, refusing to look at her friend. "I heard there was a new virus going around."

"Sara, this is me you're talking to," Tess practically hissed in an attempt to keep her voice down. "You are not the type to faint because of the heat, a virus or anything. You passed out for a very good reason, and I want to know what it was." She crossed her arms in front of her, prepared to stay until she heard the whole story.

"Well, I can tell you I'm not pregnant," she quipped.

Tess rolled her eyes. "That isn't funny and you know it. You're not the type to faint."

"Even in this modern day and age it is perfectly acceptable to faint."

Tess looked skeptical. "I'll get Tim to take you home, and I'll be over tomorrow to talk," she assured her. She opened the door to find the boy hovering outside. "She seems to have a low-grade fever," she lied without a qualm, saying it loud enough for all the sharp ears nearby. "Why don't you take her home for some rest?"

Tim nodded and rushed to help his mother to her feet.

"Tim, I can walk," she assured him with a wan smile.

He refused to listen to her protests and helped her outside to the car and drove out of the parking lot as if he was transporting a precious cargo.

Tim helped her to her bedroom and suggested she lie down while he got her something cool to drink. Jackson pounded on the closed bedroom door demanding to know what was wrong and finally retreated when Tim told him Sara had fainted in church and needed peace and quiet.

"Maybe you should take a nap," Tim suggested nervously, clearly unused to seeing his mother ill, since Sara hadn't been sick a day in her life as far as he remembered.

She flashed him a reassuring smile. "I think I will. Thank you." Her smile disappeared when the door closed behind her son. She got up off the bed and slipped off her dress, putting on her robe before lying back on top of the bed with the pillows propped up behind her.

How could this happen? After all these years Jess showed up in her town and just by his presence threatened to blow her secret sky-high when she had carefully nurtured it for so long.

"Mom is my daddy dead?"

"No, honey, he's just far away."

"Will he ever come to see me?"

"I'm afraid not."

"Mom, what's a bastard?"

"A very nasty word, and I don't want to hear you use it."

"Then why do the kids at school call me that?"

"Because they don't understand."

"Understand what?"

"A lot of things. I only wish I could tell you so you could understand. Someday I will. I promise."

Only she hadn't. At least, she hadn't said enough to truly explain what had happened sixteen years ago.

How do you tell a boy you had fallen in love with his father, made love with him and created a new life? And because of her immaturity and pride, she hadn't contacted her lover to let him know he was a father until it was too late. By then no one knew where he was.

"Mom, I hate my father. It isn't right you have to work so hard. It isn't right. If he was here, I would kill him. I would!"

The sad part was that Sara believed Tim. One day she and Jackson had talked about her few years at school and what she had given up by not being able to return to school to get her degree. That was the first time she had talked about that period of her life, and unfortunately Tim had overheard the conversation. His anger toward the unknown man increased even more after that.

Sara closed her eyes. She had thought her life was settling down nicely. She had even thought again about selling the station and moving to a larger town. The trouble was she virtually had no skills, and she knew Jackson wouldn't leave Henderson, and she certainly couldn't leave him behind. No one else would take care of the feisty old coot, and he had lived in her house for so long she considered him part of the family. He may not have been the most appropriate paternal substitute for Tim, but he was always there whenever the boy needed him, and Tim did listen to him.

Sara thought back to that moment in the church when her eyes had met astonished dark brown ones. He had looked just as shocked as she felt. The years had treated Jess kindly. His body was still lean and rangy, his hair still dark with only scattered strands of gray. She smothered a laugh threatening to erupt from her throat. Jess Larkin a preacher; her wild, unconcerned-with-propriety lover was now a preacher. From the first time she had met him she knew he walked a fine line regarding the law, but she had still loved him, because he had never done anything to frighten her. No, he only loved her as much as she had loved him. Well, it appeared he had finally tumbled off that line and the direction he had taken was unexpected. What had prompted him to go into the ministry? There had to be a good story behind that, but she wasn't about to hear it. Henderson was a small town, so she would be unable to avoid him all the time, and she certainly couldn't change churches without causing questions, so she would just go about her business as before. After all, she wasn't the newcomer here. Besides, the town's minister wouldn't want to have anything to do with the town's scarlet woman.

Surprisingly Sara did eventually fall asleep. But her dreams were punctuated with scenes from the past.

The first time she had met Jess she had been a waitress in a coffee shop near the college, and he had come in late one night looking as dangerous as the world outside the cozy confines of the restaurant. She had left with him when her shift was over and never looked back.

Jess had been a rebel then in every sense of the word. He thought everyone over the age of twenty-five was the enemy even though he was the ripe old age of twenty-two, and he had no use for anything that hinted of convention. And Sara, who knew so little about life and love, adored him. She thought he was everything she wanted, and oh, how she was going to reform him! She would graduate from college, get a good job, make sure Jess finished school, and they would marry, buy a house and have children. Only one item on her list came true.

She just hadn't realized that Jess didn't have the same dreams.

What prompted him to become a preacher? The question nagged in her brain. Had the outlaw decided a more-than-conventional life was for him? And who accomplished what she never could?

Sara tossed and turned in her bed until midafternoon. When she finally awoke, she had a hazy memory of Tim knocking on her door and asking if she was all right then the door opening softly and closing just as carefully.

All too soon she would have to sit Tim down and have a long talk with him about his father. The day of reckoning was rapidly approaching. She could feel it in her bones.

JESS WAS DOING quite a bit of thinking about Sara that same afternoon. After a hearty meal of good old-fashioned Southern fried chicken, mashed potatoes and a slice of berry pie, Reverend Mapes retired to his room for a nap, and Jess fixed himself a large glass of iced tea and wandered out to the backyard to lounge in the hammock that hung under two leafy trees. It was just as hot in the shade as in the sun, but he didn't care. He had a lot of things to think over, and he preferred being outside to do it.

Sara here. How ironic to see her after all these years. He recalled how he had hated her in the beginning for leaving him without a word, and then thoughts of her were relegated to the back of his mind as he concentrated on his studies, and later his first preaching position took precedence.

Oh, there were times when some little thing would bring her memory to the surface, and he would wonder what she was doing, but that was all. A love as young as theirs had been couldn't survive sixteen years. In fact the few times he did think of her he would figure she'd gotten married and had children. He even pictured her pleasingly plump with four children, a large shaggy dog, a station wagon and a husband who made her happy. Instead of four, he only saw one child and no husband, and she certainly wasn't plump, but still pleasing to the eye. Reverend Mapes had told him the boy was Sara's fifteen-year-old son, and there had never been a husband. A boy who looked very much like Jess had at that age. The idea shook him badly. The older man intimated that some of the townspeople condemned Sara for keeping her son, and while he hadn't voiced his own views, Jess read easily between the lines. Reverend Mapes thought a great deal of Sara and felt she had been hurt enough in the past without taking on any more.

He stretched out, looking up at the tree that shaded this corner of the yard. A part of him wanted to rush over to her and ask if the boy was his. Was he a result of one of those nights that had been so beautiful for the two of them? He would probably never know. Besides, what if she told him no? How would he feel if the boy wasn't his, because his age would mean she had gone to someone else right after leaving him? While the knowledge wouldn't hurt him after all this time, he still wasn't sure if he wanted to know such brutal truth.

Jess had lived around enough small-minded people over the years to see that Sara wasn't considered the most popular woman in town. He had seen how coldly many of the older women had treated her, and he felt angry toward these people. He also knew it wouldn't be long before conflicting stories about Sara and her son would be filtering his way. And there would be a few who would hope he would judge her just as harshly as they did. He grimaced.

That was the problem with small towns. Everyone had to put their two cents in. And with him being single, he wouldn't have it easy. He had already received several invitations to dine at various congregation members' homes. He wouldn't be surprised if he would find an unmarried daughter, niece or granddaughter in the house. He proudly admitted to himself he'd stayed free this long, so it would take a pretty stubborn lady to catch him now. With that thought his eyes drifted shut, and he dozed on and off for the rest of the afternoon.

SARA WANTED TO PLUNGE right into the morning. Last night's quiet had given her too much time to think, time to think about things better left forgotten, about dreams that had been shelved.

Sara'd had her share of dreams, a wish to teach high-school history, to travel all over the world during school vacations, to have a nice home and family. Instead she was running a gas station and working on cars in order to make a decent living. Her once-lovely slim hands were callused and rough, her nails kept short out of necessity and her long hair only trimmed when she thought of it. No wonder there were days she felt sorry for herself. But she refused to give in to self-pity for too long; there was too much to do and self-pity wasn't worth the time or effort.

Today she would fill her time with activities and people. She needed to stop reflecting on the past and all the what-might-have-beens and get on with her life.

On the way downstairs she stopped by Tim's room and knocked loudly on his door. After hearing mumbles that no human being should have to get up so early, she reminded him to strip his bed so she could put clean sheets on it and went into the kitchen. Jackson was already there drinking his first cup of coffee.

"Is breakfast ready?" Tim asked, entering the large room. "I'm starved."

"You're always starved," Sara retorted, taking a skillet out of a cabinet and the eggs and ham slices out of the refrigerator. "How many eggs do you want?"

"Five or six."

"Tim, you're eating me out of house and home."

He grinned, a grin her battered heart told her was the image of his father's. Damn, how was she going to handle this? "I'm just a growing boy, remember?"

She looked at the T-shirt straining over his rapidly broadening shoulders. "Unfortunately, I do."

Tim wolfed down his breakfast and left with a vague wave of his hand.

"Try and go to school today," she called after him. "You just might like it."

But by then Tim was out of earshot; she was sure it was intentional. Sara sighed as she got up with the dirty dishes and set them in the sink for washing. Usually she rinsed them off and waited to wash them at lunchtime. This time she decided to get them done now. Besides it gave her something to do while she talked to Jackson, and she wouldn't have to worry about looking at him directly.

"Jackson, I may have to leave town," she told him in a low voice, staring down at the plate she was slowly washing with a soapy dishcloth.

"Why?"

She drew in a deep breath. She wasn't going to be able to put him off with a fabricated story; Jackson could see through the most intricate of lies. "The new minister is Tim's father," she said quickly before she lost her courage.

"Well, I'll be damned," he breathed.

"At the rate you're going I don't think you have anything to worry about," she said wryly, setting the clean dish aside and picking up Jackson's dirty dishes.

He grinned. "As long as I know I'll find all my friends down there I'll die a happy man." He sobered. "What're you gonna do?"

She shrugged. "I have no idea. But if the wrong people find out, it could ruin Jess's reputation, and I couldn't do that to him."

"Not even after what he did to you?" Jackson sputtered.

"It was a two-way street, Jackson. We both were wrong, and we were too young. Right now I'm just going to wait and see what happens."

"What if he comes after you?"

"He won't."

"How do you know?"

"He didn't before, why should he now?" she said softly. "And maybe if I'm lucky, he won't realize that Tim's his son, and I won't have to worry about a thing."

Jackson didn't look convinced as he muttered he better get down to the station to open up. As he opened the door, he turned back to look at her. "Girl, I'm always here," he said gruffly, then hurried out the door.

"You wonderful old man," she murmured, trying hard not to cry in the dishwater as she finished her washing up.

When Sara arrived at the station, Jackson was putting the final touches on a car that had been left there the previous day. Their days were usually pretty busy, not slacking off until midmorning. At first she furtively watched each car pulling up to the pumps for fear Jess would appear. She knew she wasn't ready to see him again just yet, even though it would eventually have to happen. In a town this size and with only the one gas station there was no way out.

She had finally relaxed and was sitting in the garage chatting with Jackson while he worked when the outside bell chimed.

"You're in charge of the pumps today," Jackson told her, not looking up from the engine he was working on.

"Slave driver," she grumbled, rising to her feet and sauntering outside. She shaded her eyes with her hand as she walked down to the pumps. She didn't recognize the fairly new Ford Bronco and wondered who'd bought himself a new truck. It wasn't until the driver climbed out and walked around to the pump side that she momentarily froze. The bright sunlight turned into a gray haze surrounding her.

The eyes, the hair, the angular features, the lean body she once knew as well as her own appeared the same. The only difference was the absence of sheer arrogance in his manner. The young man once determined to take the world by storm seemed to have grown up.

Haven't we all? she thought drily as she approached him. "Reverend," she said as coolly as possible as she opened the gas cap and inserted the nozzle in one smooth motion. "Do you want the tank filled?"

"Hello, Sara." His voice was deeper than she remembered and music to her ears. Except it was a song she would have preferred to have kept in the back of her mind. "Yes, I would, thank you."

She was grateful he didn't offer to do it himself. She needed something to keep her hands busy, or she would definitely scream at him, demand that he stay away from her and her son. Those thoughts were more than enough to strengthen her backbone. Her face remained calm, her eyes blank. She could have been confronting a complete stranger instead of an old lover and the father of her child.

Jess's thoughts ran along the same vein as he watched the fragile-looking woman move about. She hadn't changed a bit, except in her manner to him. This was not the laughing girl who used to greet him every day. Judging from the faint lines of strain around her lips, she hadn't had much occasion to smile lately. He found it difficult to believe Sara had a teenage son, *their* son. Why hadn't she tried to contact him? He silently admitted there wasn't an ironclad guarantee that the boy was his, but he remembered the old Sara, and he couldn't imagine she would have gone from him to someone else. What they had shared had been too special for her to dismiss him so casually. Although, he reminded himself, she had left without a word to him; that could certainly be considered a casual dismissal. No, that wasn't Sara. There had to be something else. Questions about Sara and her son had been nagging him for the past twenty-four hours, and he hoped to have some answers soon. Right now he doubted he would get anything from the tight-lipped woman standing nearby. So instead he leaned against the hood of his truck and watched her, storing up new mental pictures to compare with the old.

Her shirt was loose fitting but not so loose he couldn't tell that her breasts were fuller, but still high and firm. Was that because of the pregnancy? Had she breastfed her baby? He could smell the warm clean fragrance of her skin, since she wore no perfume. Her wrists were so tiny he could have circled them with his fingers, her throat was equally delicate. He had always been so careful with her, afraid he would hurt her if his lovemaking was too rough, or that he might be too heavy on top of her, but all she ever told him was that she loved everything that had to do with him. So if she loved him that much, why did she leave without a word? Why had she run away?

Sara was never so relieved as when the pump clicked off. She pulled the nozzle out and twisted the gas cap back on. Every nerve ending in her body was screaming out at the man standing nearby. She knew her feelings for him were dead, but that didn't stop her from wondering what his activities had been during the past sixteen years. Especially what had turned him around so completely from the hellion she had known so long ago. Of course she couldn't remember seeing all that many ministers dressed the way he was. Wearing a pair of faded jeans slung low on his lean hips, an equally faded blue-and-gray flannel shirt and scuffed cowboy boots, he looked far from the part of a small-town preacher. Now he looked more like the rebellious Jess she remembered and had once loved.

"Why, Sara?" Jess's voice was so low the words floated in the air before reaching her ears.

She spun around, her body stiff with anger. There was no pretending she hadn't understood the meaning of the question. "Why?" Her voice vibrated with the tension she felt inside. "After what had happened between us, I think you know very well why." She glanced at the pump. "That will be twelve dollars and sixty-eight cents."

"Sara, we need to talk." His voice was low and compelling. He wanted an answer, but she wasn't going to supply one. He reached out to grasp her hand, but she stepped back before he could touch her.

"We have nothing to talk about."

"Nothing? You can say that after what we once had?" he demanded, his brows drawn together in a frown.

Her laugh was harsh and very bitter. "Had. That's the operative word, Jess. A lot of things have changed since then. You're going to be our highly revered minister, and many of the town's good ladies would call me a scarlet woman. Those two don't exactly go together."

Jess's face paled. He stepped forward and grabbed her arm, holding it in an inflexible grip. What had happened over the years to make her so bitter? "Don't ever call yourself that," he ordered harshly.

"Around here you learn to call it like it is," she spat out. "Now if you don't mind, I'd like the twelve sixty-eight." She looked up and stepped away from his grasp when a pickup roared into the other side of the pumps and screeched to a stop.

"Hi there, sweet thing." Albert climbed out of the truck and reached for the pump, all the time keeping his eyes on Jess. "How 'bout you and me taking a drive out to the lake?"

"How about you taking a drive out to the lake by yourself," she suggested, taking the money from Jess and walking up to the office to get his change.

"You're new around here. I'm Albert Patterson," Albert commented, after watching Sara walk away and muttering a crude comment about her body.

"Yes, I am." Jess tamped down the sudden rush of anger at the other man. Is this what she meant? No one should have to put up with idiots like this man. No wonder she was so bitter.

Albert narrowed his eyes as he studied Jess. There was something about this man that bothered him; he wasn't sure if it was the way he looked at him or what. He just knew he didn't like him. He looked beyond Jess at the fairly new Bronco.

"Sara's not what you want if you're looking for a *nice* lady." Albert's smile held a slight leer. "If you know what I mean."

Jess's face didn't change expression, but there was still something in the dark features that left Albert feeling unnerved.

"'Judge not lest ye be judged,'" he quoted.

Albert looked blank. "What?"

By this time Sara had returned and handed Jess his change. She looked at the two men, aware of some sort of tension emanating from them.

Jess smiled. "Matthew, chapter seven, verse one. To further clarify it for you, it's a verse from the Bible. Oh, yes, I'm afraid I forgot to introduce myself. I'm Pastor Larkin. I'll be taking over for Pastor Mapes. Come to think of it, I met a Mrs. Albert Patterson yesterday. I gather she's your wife?" He turned to Sara, giving her a smile that warned her their conversation was far from finished. "Thank you, Miss Murdock. I'll see you on Sunday." He looked at Albert. "You, too, Mr. Patterson." He climbed into the truck and drove away.

Albert scowled at the cloud of dust. "Who the hell does he think he is?" he muttered.

"He told you," Sara replied, keeping her pleased smile hidden. It was a rare moment to see someone show Albert what a fool he really was, and she was glad she had been present for the occasion. "He's taking over for Pastor Mapes." She glanced at the pump that had clicked off. "My, my, you must have been doing a lot of driving lately. Eighteen dollars even."

His scowl deepened. "I only wanted five dollars' worth," he argued.

"Then you should have told me instead of gassing your truck up yourself," she pointed out mildly, holding out her hand.

"It was because of that damn preacher," he muttered, dragging out his wallet and carefully counting out the bills. "What the hell did he mean about meeting my wife?" he spat, for once forgetting his obsession with teasing Sara every time he came to the station.

"I think he was talking about meeting Sharon at church, that's all," Sara said airily, pocketing the money. "You have a good day, Albert." She almost skipped back up to the garage, feeling more light-hearted than she had in a long time.

"What was goin' on out there?" Jackson asked, standing in the doorway, wiping his greasy hands on an equally greasy rag.

"Albert finally got a bit of his own back," she chuckled, walking into the office and putting away the money.

"Don't forget he can get mean if he's crossed," he warned. "I sure wouldn't like to see you on the wrong end of his temper." His rough features lightened. "'Course, I don't think that other fella will worry about it." His sharp eyes speared her. "So that's Tim's daddy."

Sara flushed. "How did you know?"

"All I had to do was look at the man after what you'd already told me. Did he ask you anything about Tim?"

On the outside she may have looked unconcerned, but on the inside she was shaking like a leaf. "He had nothing to say that I might want to hear." She peered into the garage. "Do you have Mr. Roberts's car finished yet? He should be by for it pretty soon, and you know how he hates to wait."

"It's done, and I don't like you changing the subject on me. I care about what happens to you, girl, and I'll do anything I physically can to make sure you don't end up hurt from all this."

Sara knew he meant it and resisted the urge to hug him knowing Jackson would only put her off with his usual gruff temperament.

"Just tell me one thing," he went on. "The time will probably come when Tim finds out his father is here and who he is. And when that time comes, he's going to go to you for some answers. What the hell are you going to do then?"

Sara rubbed her aching temples with her fingertips. "I don't know, Jackson," she sighed. "I just don't know."

Chapter Three

"All right, I want to hear the entire story from beginning to end, and I want nothing left out," Tess ordered, after pouring two cups of coffee and setting them on the table. They may have been in Sara's kitchen, but Tess firmly believed in making herself at home wherever she was. From the time she had arrived at the gas station ten minutes ago and informed Jackson, after leaving him with an ample supply of freshly baked cinnamon rolls, she was taking Sara up to the house for a coffee break, she hadn't paused long enough to take a breath. She rummaged around in the kitchen, found coffee makings and fixed a pot before beginning her interrogation.

Sara sipped her coffee and bit into the still-warm roll. "This is wonderful," she murmured. "I'm certainly glad you picked up your mother's knack for baking. This recipe was always my favorite, and I never could get it right. My rolls either come out too heavy or too doughy."

"Sara! What went on yesterday?" she demanded. "You're not the type to faint."

"It was awfully warm in there, and I've been so busy lately I really haven't kept up with all my meals."

Tess rolled her eyes. "Sara, this is me, remember? From the time we were three we shared all our secrets. Don't forget I have enough material on you to blackmail you for the rest of our lives. After all, I never told Mrs. Farmer that you were the one to throw up in her desk."

Sara gasped, keeping back a loud laugh. "That's right, talk about my good points," she teased. "Because if you ever bring that up in public, I'll mention that little-known fact of who was the one to take the football team's jockstraps and hang them from the flagpole during our senior year."

Tess wrinkled her nose. "Don't forget I made sure their names showed."

"And everyone swore up and down that Wayne Dalton wore a size small," she giggled.

"Didn't he?" Tess hooted.

The two friends laughed as they recalled some of the more colorful memories of their youth.

"Okay, you've gotten me off the subject long enough, but no more," Tess said firmly. "What is going on?"

Sara stared down into her coffee cup, wishing it was tea with magical leaves that would tell her exactly what to do. No such luck. "Tim's father is in town," she explained in a low voice.

Tess straightened up at that piece of news. "He is? Well, when, who, why? How did he find you?"

This was the hardest to say. Tess was right; she and Sara had never kept a secret from each other all their lives, until this one. Sara had never divulged the identity of Tim's father to anyone, and Tess, being the sometimes tactful soul she could be, never asked, preferring to wait until Sara felt confident enough to tell her. She hadn't realized it would take this long.

"He arrived here a few days ago, I guess. And his name is Jess Larkin, and he's here because of a new job."

Tess shook her head. "Jess Larkin? I don't think I—" The light bulbs went off with a three-hundred-watt brilliance. "Jess Larkin, as in Reverend Jess Larkin?" Her voice squeaked toward the end.

Sara nodded. She couldn't bear to look at Tess just yet. This was hard enough to talk about as it was.

"But Sara..." Tess was finding it difficult to take it all in.

"I guess I should say that his full name is Jesse Timothy, a family name," she explained.

"Timothy...Tim..." Tess mused. Then the complications all this would involve dawned on her. "Oh, God," she breathed, downing the rest of her coffee and wishing it was something much stronger. "What...did he know you lived here?"

Sara remembered the shock in his eyes when he first saw her yesterday and shook her head. "No, he didn't know." Her face warmed. "We, ah, we never talked all that much about where we came from." No, they were much too busy with the present to worry about their pasts. They figured that would come in time. The only problem was that the time never came for them.

"Sara, talk to me about it," Tess urged, reaching across to grasp her hand. "You've held this in too long, and I'm afraid it's poisoned you."

"Tess, don't be silly." She tried to laugh it off, but it wasn't as easy as she thought, because her laughter soon turned into tears. And once they began she had no control over them. Pretty soon she laid her face down on her crossed arms and sobbed deeply.

"Sara, no," Tess moaned, swiftly getting up and going over to her friend, putting her arms around her. "You're only going to make yourself sick if you cry too much."

"I loved him so much," she sobbed. "Tess, I loved him, but he didn't love me back enough."

Tess gasped. "Sara, are you sure?"

She nodded. "He never told me he did."

"Did you ever talk to him about your feelings for him?" Tess grabbed her purse and retrieved a handkerchief, handing it to Sara.

"Not really, because I was afraid he'd laugh at me," she sniffed, accepting the fine cotton, lace-trimmed square and blowing her nose. "Oh, Tess, those months we had together were so beautiful." She straightened up in an attempt to pull herself back together. "But I loved him too much, and I wanted to get married, and he didn't." A part of her mind reminded her there was more to the story, but she refused to acknowledge it.

"All you ever told me was that you met him in the coffee shop you worked at," Tess prompted, hoping that getting her to talk about it would help.

Sara nodded. "He, ah, he came in late one night." She remembered the rainy night well. Who could forget the young man sauntering in, his overly long hair wet from the rain and silver drops decorating his black leather jacket? Her smile was wobbly. "He sat at the counter and ordered a cup of coffee and a hamburger. He wasn't one to waste any time. He asked me if I had a boyfriend, and when I said no, he asked what time I got off."

"You're right, he didn't waste any time," Tess said drily, refilling their coffee cups and pushing another roll in front of Sara. "Was he a student at the college?"

"A graduate student," she replied. "But he said school wasn't really for him, although I knew he had the intelligence to do anything he wanted."

"Like Tim," Tess mused.

"Like Tim," Sara verified. She was lost in memories she hadn't dredged up for a long time. "Oh, Tess, he was so exciting. Jess could make the slightest outing seem special. Whether it was a concert, a play on campus or just a walk, he made it something more exciting for me. For the first time in my life I felt loved." Her voice broke on the last word.

Tess understood. While Sara's parents had always been careful to provide for her material needs, they ignored her emotional ones. She had been expected to do well in school and marry after graduation. That she wanted to go on to college was beyond their idea of a proper daughter. She was told if she wanted it badly enough, she would have to do it on her own, that they wouldn't throw money away on an advanced education when she wouldn't use it after she eventually married. Tess had always thought Sara's parents were cold, and as she grew older she realized they just didn't know what to do with a child, since Sara had been born to them when they were in their late forties. Tess could understand why Sara would reach out to the first person to offer her something she had never experienced before. Too bad that it almost destroyed her.

"It's going to come out in the open, Sara," Tess said gently. "You do realize that, don't you? With him here the many sharp-eyed old harpies in this town will soon see the resemblance."

"I know," Sara said wearily, pressing her fingertips against her temples to halt the headache pounding there. "That's why I thought about moving away as soon as I can sell the station."

"That sounds more like running away."

"What am I supposed to do?" she demanded. "Wait until someone like Mrs. Masterson sees the resemblance and starts her evil gossip? It would ruin Jess's reputation, and while I'm not happy about his being here, I don't wish him any harm. As for Tim, think what it would do to him. He's been so hostile regarding his father that I'm afraid he would try something we'd all regret. No, I can't allow that to happen."

"Forgive me for being so crass but did you ever stop to think that no one will talk as long as you stay away from him? After all, Sara, who's going to make the connection?"

"After seeing Jess today I don't think he'll let it rest. He's a very stubborn man."

"To be honest, you sound as if you still have some feelings for him."

Sara shook her head. "Not really. They ended a long time ago."

"True," Tess agreed. "After all, you're both different people now, but you can't tell me you don't wonder why he never tried to find you."

Sara stared down at the table. "I hate people who can be so logical," she mumbled, silently admitting she had wondered that.

"So does Charlie, but he likes my pot roast, so he has to keep me around." Tess stood up, carried her coffee cup over to the sink and rinsed it out. "Sara, don't run away," she said softly. "You and I both know Tim is going through some tough times right now, and moving won't solve them. If he finds out, then it's meant to happen, and perhaps it's for the best for all of you. As for Jess's reputation and career, that'll be his problem, not yours.''

"I should have married Ralph."

Tess threw her hands up. "You would have been bored in five seconds. Sara, the man had no personality and no brain. His idea of a fun evening was sitting outside watching the grass grow. Besides, the only reason he wanted to marry you was because he felt Tim needed a father influence, and you know it.''

"If Tim had had a father all along, he might not be on a first-name basis with half the police force in the county.''

"Hey, look at the bright side. He might grow up to be a cop." She smiled. "Just remain calm and everything will end up fine, you'll see.''

"Thank you, Aunt Tess. Do you have any other words of advice for me?''

"Yes. Stop acting sorry for yourself and give the guy a chance if he wants to talk to you about what happened back then. You just might be surprised.''

"Tess, when I met Jess, he was walking a fine line with the law, like someone else we know. Several people at school warned me about him, saying he only cared for himself and refused to conform to anything that smacked of establishment. It was predicted that he would probably end up in prison one day. He didn't care about his studies and only attended class when he felt like it. Ironically several of his instructors let him get away with a great deal, because they felt he had potential and hoped the day would come when he would use it.'' Her lips curved in a mirthless smile. "If only they could see him now.''

"I wonder what caused such a radical change in him," Tess commented, wrapping aluminum foil around the rolls and setting them on the counter. "No man goes from one extreme to the other without a good reason."

"I really don't care."

Tess smiled at Sara's careless words. "I think you do. You're just too stubborn to admit it. We're having a barbecue Saturday night, so put it on your social calendar. You need to get out more. Tim is more than welcome if he doesn't mind being around grown-ups and little monsters, and so is Jackson if he cares to be sociable."

"Sounds good. I'll bring a salad and dessert."

"Make something sinful," Tess advised with a saucy wink. "I'm sure I'll see or talk to you before then. Take care, Sara." She walked over to her and hugged her tightly.

After Tess left, Sara sat back down at the table, thinking about the first time she and Jess had made love. She had been so frightened, not of the act, but at the idea of Jess laughing at her obvious inexperience. But he hadn't laughed, instead he told her how much he cherished her and that he would never hurt her. They lay in his bed, the covers trailing down to the floor and talked about what their futures would be like. From the beginning Jess had taken great care in protecting her from pregnancy, until that one night. How clear it remained in her mind.

"I didn't think it could happen!" she had cried out. "I thought nothing could go wrong."

"Honey, I'm sorry, but it broke," he told her, taking her in his arms. She had cried, fearing the worst, and he had comforted her the best way he knew how.

"Don't worry, I'll take care of you if... well, if... you know."

Yes, she knew ten weeks later, but she had left Jess by then, and her stubborn nature refused to allow her to contact him.

Sara had felt so bitter and hurt regarding Jess back then.

"Hey, you gonna stay up here all day, or you comin' back to help me?" Jackson growled from the open back door. "I'm an old man, you know. I can't do everything at once."

Sara knew better, but she would allow him his grumbling. "Jackson, you can do more than a man half your age, and you know it." She glanced at the clock on the microwave and stood up. "How about some lunch first?"

"We have any ham left?"

"Yes. Does that mean ham sandwiches are all right?"

"Only with lots of mustard. You never use enough."

Sara grimaced as she brought out the sandwich makings and took a loaf of sourdough out of the bread keeper. "Your idea of lots of mustard is three-quarters of the jar." She set everything on the counter and reached into the cabinet for plates. "Any business?"

"A couple people for gas. Someone else stopping by for directions, so don't count your first million just yet."

Sara quickly assembled a sandwich for herself and two for Jackson and carried the coffeepot over to the table.

"Does the bastard know what kinda hell you've been through all these years, thanks to him?" Jackson ate half his sandwich in one neat bite.

"Last I heard ministers worked to keep you out of hell, not put you there. Besides, I put myself there. He had nothing to do with it."

He muttered under his breath, careful that Sara didn't hear the exact wording.

"What're you going to tell Tim?" he demanded.

"Nothing."

"He might find out."

"I doubt it," she replied calmly. "Who would connect the pious Reverend Larkin with someone like me?" Bitterness laced her words.

"It won't be difficult as long as he looks at you like you're the damn blue-plate special at Elsie's Diner," he rumbled, attacking his second sandwich with gusto. "Dammit, Sara, there's hardly no mustard on this thing!"

Sara toyed with the end of her braid. "Your language and your grammar get worse every day. By rights you should have your mouth washed out with soap. Except that I'd go through at least two bars of soap a day."

"At my age I can say anything I damn well please without answering to anyone," he said smugly, pleased to be one up on her. "That's why I never married. I didn't want some woman messing up my life." He grinned wickedly at her.

Sara rolled her eyes. "No wonder Tim talks as if he lived in a locker room when you're his only example."

"I remember you calling the washer some pretty nasty names a week ago," he pointed out, still smug.

"The longer I know you, the more I understand why Harvey threatened to murder you at least once a day," she attacked without venom. Their playful arguments were part of a way of life in the Murdock household.

"He wasn't all that easy to get along with, either," Jackson reminded her, a strange note in his voice as he thought about his closest friend.

Sara thought about the gruff man who rarely had a kind word for anyone, but who hadn't thought twice when a young girl needed a roof over her head. Harvey Carson had loudly claimed more than once that he would never allow a woman into his house and thought the institution of marriage was just that, an institution. Yet he waited on Sara hand and foot during the last months of her pregnancy and insisted she lift nothing heavier than a handkerchief. It was thanks to his straightforward common sense and his and Jackson's squabbling that she was able to retain her sanity instead of wondering what had gone wrong with her young life. For that she was thankful.

After lunch they returned to their separate duties. Jackson decided it was time to work on his truck, and Sara remained at the house to do some cleaning. It didn't take her long to have the two bathrooms sparkling and the rooms dusted and beds fitted with clean sheets. She had to do anything she could to keep Jess from her mind. What was she going to do? How could she attend church every Sunday and look up at the man sermonizing and remember how he once looked naked in her bed?

Sara's laughter held a hysterical note, the towels dropping from her nerveless hands. That was one memory she preferred to keep buried deep. How many times had they just lain together in bed talking about their dreams? Jess's skin was always so warm under her fingertips that she never tired of touching him. Just the way he never tired of touching her, as if he couldn't get enough of her. She had done so well putting him out of her life that his return wasn't something she could handle very well. And she couldn't understand why. The feelings were dead and gone. Her heart had told her that. So why did her head ask so many questions?

"I'M GLAD YOU WERE ABLE to come out here ahead of time," Reverend Mapes told Jess that same afternoon as they sat together in the large study where Reverend Mapes wrote his sermons and met with members of his congregation. The elderly man watched his replacement with eyes not entirely dimmed from age. He knew Jess was troubled by something and had a vague idea what it might be, but decided to allow Jess to initiate the conversation. "You'll find out that smaller towns are different in their outlook than the big cities, because we tend to have more get-togethers and every kind of bake and rummage sale imaginable. People out here help each other." He smiled. "Being unmarried you'll also be invited to dinner a great deal, and I'm sure the single women are already planning their strategies."

Jess looked up. He'd already counted the roses in the faded carpet once, and he didn't intend to do it again. Lounging in the easy chair in his jeans and cotton shirt, he didn't look the picture of a typical small-town minister.

"The woman who fainted yesterday," he said abruptly. "I gathered from comments she isn't one of the town's leading citizens. Why?"

Reverend Mapes stared into eyes that reminded him of another pair of eyes. This pair serene, the other angry with the world. He prayed one man would be able to help the other. The more he looked, the more he was positive the resemblance was not sheer coincidence.

"Sara Murdock," he spoke slowly. "A very lovely woman who grew up here. She's always had a smile and a kind word for everyone. Her family goes back several generations, and she's always been proud of that, although considering her parents it says a lot on how certain characteristics can skip a generation."

"Why?"

The older man sighed. "Tom and Alice Murdock were very active in the church, and Alice could be counted on for bringing a casserole to someone ill or setting up a baby shower, but she didn't do it out of the goodness of her heart. She did it because it was the right thing to do." Reverend Mapes continued, telling his new minister about Sara's life with her parents and of her dreams to achieve, to learn, to go away to college.

Jess moved restively in his chair. He had a pretty good idea where this story was leading, and as he knew parts Reverend Mapes didn't, he wasn't sure if he wanted to hear the parts *he* didn't know.

The reverend shook his head, looking sad. "I called in a few favors to help her receive a scholarship, and she did very well her first two years. When she suddenly returned and explained she had dropped out of school, her parents said it was a shame she wasted all that time in school when her learning would never be used. When she discovered she was pregnant, the reaction was much worse. Her parents, well, they tried their best, but they just couldn't handle the idea that their little girl had gotten into trouble. She made the decision on her own to move out to relieve the tension in the household."

Jess looked pained. "How did she live?" His voice was husky. Why hadn't she called him? Then he remembered. Judging from the time frame, there was no way she could have gotten hold of him, unless she had tried his parents, and they had written him off long before then.

Reverend Mapes recounted the story of old man Carson, as well as the opinion of some of the town's elderly women. "Actually I think if it could have been done, they would have run her out of town on a rail. Instead, she told them her roots were here, she wanted her son's roots to be here, and she wasn't leaving just because they didn't like her presence. It hasn't been easy for her, but she never quit. I give her a lot of credit for sticking when she could have just as easily run away."

Jess did too. "Did she ever talk about the boy's father?" He stared back down at the carpet.

"No, she never did. She's had a few marriage proposals in the past. Unfortunately a couple of them didn't want Tim, and she refused to give him up. It's a shame that the boy has generated so much anger over the years," he commented. "He's angry at the world and angry at the people here for treating his mother the way they do."

"The boy, what's he like?" Jess had a faint memory of a tall boy standing next to Sara yesterday, his shock when she had fainted and how careful he was with her as they left the church.

"Tim has the brains to go far. Sara told me he scored very high in all the tests, but he doesn't have the motivation to get somewhere. Probably because the teachers think he's a lost cause and won't work with him enough. But he cares a great deal for his mother." The older man smiled. "Deep down he's a good boy, the trouble is few people care to find that out."

Jess flinched. The story sounded all too familiar.

Reverend Mapes hesitated until the younger man lifted his eyes. "Who knows, you might be the one to show him the way."

Jess's lips curved in a slight smile. "I think I'd like that," he said softly, remembering another man long ago who had shown him the way. Perhaps this was his chance to say a very special thank-you to that man.

"TIM, YOU CANNOT GO OUT tonight!" Sara informed him tautly, watching her son drag on his denim jacket.

"My homework's done."

"That's not the point! Mrs. Williams called today. She said you're failing history and English. If you don't bring your grades up by the end of the quarter, they will have no choice but to expel you."

"Good. Then maybe I can do something useful with my life instead of wasting it in school." His face tightened with the inner anger he had carried for so long it seemed a part of him.

"If you want to do something useful, study harder to get your grades up!" she shouted, her hands braced on her hips. "If you need help, I'll do anything I can. Dammit, don't do this!"

Tim turned away. He didn't like to upset her. He did love his mother and wanted to do anything he could for her, but she couldn't understand why he hated school so much, and he didn't want to tell her and see the pain fill her face. She would think it was her fault, and he refused to allow that to happen. Instead he preferred to spend his evenings with guys who didn't care he was a screwup. Maybe they weren't the kind his mom would approve of, but they knew how to have a good time. A part of him wondered if Lora Summers would care who he was. The trouble was, he was too afraid to find out.

He already saw what kind of guys hung around her, and he doubted he would be welcome. But he knew where he was and that was where he was going.

"Tim, please, stay home. Let's talk things over. I'm so afraid for you being out so much with those boys. I don't want to see you get into any trouble." Sara's voice throbbed with emotion. She felt as if she were on the verge of tears, and the feeling overwhelmed her. She put a hand out, but he moved away before she could touch him.

He stood with his back to her, his hands braced on his hips, his head bowed in thought. "Don't sweat it."

"But I do worry about you, dammit!" Sara turned away, grateful that Jackson was at his weekly poker game. She didn't think she was up to hearing his well-intentioned advice. She didn't move when denim-covered arms circled her waist and a familiar chin rested on the top of her head.

"Mom, I do love you," he said quietly. "You know that, but I'm not getting anywhere here. That's not your fault," he added hastily. "It's mine."

"I'm glad to see you realize that," she murmured. She wondered how Tim could make her so angry one moment and close to tears the next. "So why are you trying to make me so crazy?"

He chuckled. "It's the age, Mom. Don't you read any of those why-is-my-kid-doing-this-to-me articles?"

She turned around. "You have so much potential, Tim. I just want to see you make good use of it."

"Oh, come on, that's what school counselors hand out to all the parents so they won't know how dumb their kid really is," he argued.

She placed her hands on his arms, surprised at the muscle underneath the jacket. When had this happened? she asked herself. How could he have grown up without her knowing it? Was she the kind of mother who preferred remembering him in little sailor suits and riding a tricycle?

"I just don't want us to grow apart," she said softly, not caring if her fears were revealed so blatantly.

He hesitated. Part of him still wanted to go out. Not necessarily to get into trouble, but to be with other misfits like himself. He knew if he went now he wouldn't enjoy himself, because he'd remember how hurt his mother looked.

"If anyone finds out I stayed home because you wanted me to, I'd lose my reputation," he muttered, with a scowl on his face.

Her lips quivered with a fleeting smile. "I won't ask you to play Monopoly."

Chapter Four

Sara made sure she kept herself busy so she couldn't think about Jess. When the evening of Tess and Charlie's barbecue came around, she felt more than ready to relax and enjoy herself in the company of her friends. Their large two-story house in the center of town always looked the same with its various toys and bicycles littering the front yard showing the friendly neglect of a family who preferred spending time with each other instead of working in the yard to keep it well manicured.

Sara withdrew a pasta salad and chocolate-chip cheesecake from her car's passenger seat and carried her contributions to the barbecue around to the back of the house where she could hear sounds of children squealing and adults chattering in loud voices. Her eyes widened when she saw what amounted to a small crowd scattered throughout the backyard.

"Sara, hi!" One woman greeted her with a broad smile. "Oh my God, you made that sinful cheesecake, didn't you? There goes the diet, because there's no way I'll be able to stay away from it."

"Don't worry, Maggie, I always bake the calories out of it," she teased the woman, another classmate. She glanced warily around at the other guests, although she knew she had nothing to worry about. She had gone to school with a majority of the people present and knew they didn't look upon her with scorn the way most of the town's older residents did.

After setting the dishes on a counter in the kitchen and greeting several other women, Sara wandered back outside.

"Hey, lady, no one is allowed here without a drink." Charlie handed her a glass of white wine and pressed a kiss on her cheek at the same time. "How ya doing?"

She sipped the cool liquid and smiled her thanks. "Better now." She glanced around. "Tess didn't tell me you were having an all-out bash tonight."

"She knew if she did, you wouldn't come."

"She was right." Sara nodded and smiled at several people who called out to her. She noted a volleyball net set up at the edge of the yard with a lively game between six men going on and children splashing in the aboveground pool set in another corner. When Tess and Charlie had bought the house several years before, Charlie had the yard landscaped into a place ideal for children to play in safely. And as Tess and Charlie enjoyed entertaining and had the room to do it, they hosted a great many parties that involved entire families.

Sara's gaze swept the area, then swung back to the improvised volleyball court where the six men were divided in teams of three. One man in particular kept her attention. Jess was on one of those teams. She found herself silently cataloging the differences between the young man she'd once known and loved and the mature man he'd grown into. His bare shoulders were broader, his once-smooth chest now dusted with crisp, dark brown hair, his body was leaner and lightly muscled. She watched the muscles in his shoulders knot when he leapt up to spike the ball over the net. When the other team failed to send it back, he laughed and cheered with his teammates. Sara could see a sheen of sweat on his upper body from his exertions. Her mouth went dry, and she quickly swallowed some wine.

"If you're going to guzzle it that way, I'm going to replace our good wine with an extremely inferior brand." Tess appeared behind her and looked in the same direction as Sara's gaze. "Charlie ran into him at the hardware store yesterday and invited him," she murmured, adding quickly when Sara turned to her, "I never told him a thing. I love my husband dearly, but he does tend to stick his foot in his mouth at times. Sara, are you sure the feelings are gone?"

She nodded, understanding her friend's concern for her. "Yes, they died a natural death a long time ago. We're not the same people we were then." She turned her back on the game so Jess wouldn't find her watching him.

Tess put her arm around her friend's shoulders and steered her back to the kitchen. "Come on, you can help some of us get the food ready. Jenny's here, so we can catch up on the latest gossip."

Inside the large country-style kitchen three other women were taking wrappers off the food dishes and dipping spoons in various bowls. In no time Sara's spirits were revived as she was put to work cutting up tomatoes and shredding lettuce for the hamburgers. Still, in the back of her mind, she recalled the man jumping up to spike the ball over the net. She began to wonder if those feelings were dead after all. She quickly roused herself, knowing this wasn't the time to think about it.

JESS HAD SEEN HER watching him. In a rare spirit of that old-fashioned macho desire to show off he had jumped up to spike the ball and looked her way out of the corner of his eye when his team congratulated him on the winning point. She wasn't dressed in jeans tonight but a pale lilac sundress with spaghetti straps. Her fair hair was twisted on top of her head in deference to the heat. The lovely girl had grown up into a lovelier woman, and he wouldn't be human if he didn't notice it. He had stopped thinking about might-have-been years ago, but seeing Sara again revived a few of those old memories, the sweet with the bitter. When he saw Tess approach Sara and walk with her into the house, he returned to the game with his usual vigor.

In the two short weeks Jess had been in town he had already gleaned a lot of information about Sara. Ninety-nine per cent of the older residents, especially the women, treated Sara with the same courtesy they would have treated Typhoid Mary. Some of the men, especially the young and cocky ones, treated her as if she ran a red-light district. He also learned she had friends, very few but extremely loyal to her.

While there were a total of twenty people, excluding the children, Sara and Jess couldn't ignore each other. She couldn't help wondering what people would say if they knew about her and Jess's shared past. At first she was afraid someone would guess the truth by some divine intuition, then laughed at her groundless fears. There was no reason for them to know. Not unless she was stupid enough to say something.

Sara wasn't surprised when she and Jess ended up sharing a table with two other couples. In fact she had a sneaking suspicion Tess had something to do with the seating arrangements and swore to get even with her later.

"Was your last church in a small town, Reverend Larkin?" she asked politely, piling lettuce, tomato and onion on her cheeseburger.

"No, I was in Atlanta," he replied, spooning a large portion of Sara's pasta salad on his plate.

"You chose to come here from Atlanta?" Suzanne, one of the other women seated at the table, looked surprised. "I hate to tell you this, but it's supposed to work the other way around." She slanted him a flirtatious glance. Newly divorced, she was known for lamenting the fact her husband had left her with little money and no means to support herself and her two small children. It was a known fact she wouldn't mind finding a second husband as soon as possible.

Jess shrugged. "I like smaller towns" was his only explanation.

While the women cleared the tables after dinner, the men moved over to a corner of the yard to talk and swap stories.

"Sara's one hell of a woman," Charlie said bluntly, after noticing on whom Jess's eyes rested the most. "She's had a few bad breaks, and quite a few people wouldn't argue if she left town for good. Yet through it all she's managed to raise her son and keep her business going." His tone was almost defiant, as if daring the minister to deny his words."

Jess shook his head. "Charlie, believe me, I'd be the last person to judge," he said quietly. "I doubt any of us were angels during our younger years. I helped run a halfway house for runaways in Atlanta that wasn't in the best part of town, and saw and heard things that could turn a strong man's stomach. Sara's a brave woman to ignore those narrow-minded few." He thought of the stormy days before they had parted and regretted his arrogance back then.

"Yeah, she's something else." Charlie sounded like the proud older brother. "It's just a shame she never married. She's got a lot to offer the right man."

Jess wondered the same thing as he wandered over to the redwood swing Sara sat on as she watched the smaller children play tag.

"Where do they get all their energy?" he wondered, sitting down beside her.

"Probably the same place we got ours when we were that age," she answered, managing to flash him a smile.

Jess closed his eyes briefly. "What about Tim?"

Her face fairly glowed in the dim light. "He ran me ragged from the time he could walk. Jackson used to say Tim couldn't sit still if his life depended on it. He's still that way," she whispered.

"What did your parents think of him?"

Sara hesitated. "They, ah, they thought he was very well mannered." She didn't want to say they saw him very few times, by their own choice.

"That isn't what I mean, and you know it," he said angrily.

She stood up and half turned to face him. "I know, but some things are easier left unsaid. My parents experienced great difficulty in knowing how to treat their grandson. Even though they lived only a mile away, I saw them rarely, and they were happier that way." Unable to say more, she stood up and held out her hand. "Good night, Reverend Larkin." She found herself desiring to put as much distance between them as possible.

Jess reached up with both his hands and clasped hers between them. "Good night, Sara." A wicked sparkle lit up his eyes. "See you in church."

Swallowing a sharp retort, Sara turned on her heel and walked swiftly away. Jess watched her speak to Tess before disappearing around the corner of the house.

"You shouldn't be sitting here all by yourself," Suzanne said brightly, dropping down beside him. Her flirtatious smile was age-old. "Now tell me all about Atlanta."

Jess's answering smile wasn't as bright. He decided if Suzanne wanted to know, he'd tell her, in great detail. With luck she wouldn't last five minutes.

WHEN SARA ARRIVED HOME she found Tim and Jackson squabbling over a poker hand.

"And I say you palmed that card!" The boy pointed an accusing finger at his partner.

"Hell, I never palmed a card in my life," Jackson blustered. "I won that hand fair and square."

Tim slumped in his chair, muttering he didn't have a chance of proving the older man cheated.

"Must be a big pot," Sara said lightly, entering the room.

"More like a useful one," Jackson chortled.

"If he wins, I have to mow the lawn for the next two months," Tim clarified when his mother turned to him.

"Now why didn't I think of gambling for your services?" she teased, looping her arms around her son's neck and dropping a kiss on his head. "I might have been lucky and had you carrying out the garbage until you were fifty."

"With the way you play poker you'd be cleaning my room for the next hundred years."

"With its present condition it would take that long." Sara leaned over to steal a potato chip. Her eyes widened at the sight of two beer bottles on the table, and she glared at Jackson.

"How was the barbecue?" the older man asked, casually pushing both bottles toward his side of the table.

"Just fine. You should have come. The new minister was there, and I'm sure the two of you could have had an enlightening conversation."

Tim choked. "Sure. Jackson could tell him why he prefers being a heathen, while the preacher could try to save him. I'd like to be there for that." He tossed down his cards. "I'm quitting."

Sara walked into the kitchen, poured herself a glass of water and carried it back to the living room.

"What's the preacher like?" Tim asked. "Did he talk about fire and brimstone during dinner?"

She shook her head. "No, he didn't, and he's like anyone else." She silently cursed herself for a stupid answer.

The boy rolled his eyes. "Come on, Mom, he's a preacher. That means no swearing, no drinking, no fooling around, basically no fun. We both know Charlie and some of the others get a little crazy when they've had a few beers in them. You forget, I used to go to some of the barbecues. Didn't they resent him being there?"

Sara thought about the old Jess who had partied with the best of them and knew he would never deliberately put a damper on someone else's fun unless it was destructive to others.

"I think he knows the difference between having a good time and having an orgy," she murmured.

Tim looked sharply at his mother. Ever since the new pastor had come to town she had been acting differently, and he didn't like it.

"Hey, why don't we go fishing tomorrow?" he spoke up. When he saw the way her face lit up at his suggestion, he felt like a heel for not doing something like this sooner. She once told him she understood he was at the age where he didn't want to be seen in public with his mother, but he sensed that didn't stop her from craving special times with him.

"That sounds like fun," she replied, trying so very hard not to sound too eager at his suggestion. "But wouldn't you have more fun if you went with some of your friends or with Jackson?"

"Probably," he replied, too candidly for her taste. "But the time's gonna come when I won't be around, so I should probably spend time with you before you're too old to have any fun."

"Thank you very much," she said wryly. "You're right, I certainly wouldn't want you to strain yourself pushing my wheelchair."

"Yeah, we talked about that kind of stuff in psychology," he explained. "I'm goin' to bed. See you in the morning."

Sara looked over at Jackson. "Why do I feel as if our fishing trip is an extra credit assignment?"

"Could be worse."

"How?"

"He could have come right out and told you it was a school assignment."

Sara winced. "If I have to get up at dawn, I better get to bed."

Within fifteen minutes she was in bed, but finding it difficult to sleep as she found herself remembering her talk with Jess and watching him play volleyball. A faint tingle flew through her veins. She dismissed it as the consequence of being alone too long and finally fell asleep after setting the alarm for what she considered an ungodly hour.

"IT'S NICE TO KNOW you haven't lost your appetite even this early in the morning," Sara said drily, watching her son demolish two stacks of pancakes and several sausage patties while she settled for a fraction of that and two cups of coffee.

She had already packed a lunch for them, and they set out on Tim's motorcycle just after dawn. She laughed out loud with pleasure as the wind whipped through her hair and they sped down the road toward the large lake on the other side of town. Tim circled the lake until he found the spot he wanted. They picked up their poles and picnic basket and made their way to the water's edge. Tim offered to bait Sara's hook with one of the worms he'd picked up at the bait shop, and they soon cast their lines out and settled down to wait for the first bite.

"I feel as if I'm being buttered up for something," Sara commented, resting against a flat rock, her pole held loosely between her fingers.

"You're too suspicious, Mom." Tim rummaged through the basket and withdrew two cans of Coke and handed one to her. "Great, you brought blueberry muffins." He grabbed one and munched away happily as if he hadn't eaten all those pancakes in the last hour.

"No, I'm practical. I know you too well." She slipped her sunglasses on when the sun began creeping upward. "So what are you angling for?"

He leaned back on his elbows gazing off into space. "A story."

She arched an eyebrow. "You were barely six when you haughtily informed me you were too old for Dr. Seuss."

Tim didn't laugh. "Do you realize you haven't joked and teased like that in a long time?"

Sara looked surprised. "What do you mean?"

"What I mean is you've turned into some kind of gloom and doom," Tim told her, turning halfway to face her. "And I think part of this is my fault." He shook his head to silence her gasp of protest. "Mom, you're not like you used to be. I can remember the way you used to laugh off the way people treated you. You don't do it anymore." His faced darkened with the same temper Sara remembered seeing on Jess's so long ago. "You always said you stayed here because you needed roots and you wanted me to have them. We could have had that somewhere else, you know, but you didn't want it. What did it get us? Creeps make passes at you, the so-called social leaders in town treat you like dirt, and when guys call me a bastard they're speaking the truth," he said bitterly.

Sara's eyes filled with tears as she reached out to grasp his hand. "Do you hate me for that? For trying to do what I mistakenly thought was right?"

"No," he hastened to reassure her. "You said you left my dad. You told the truth, didn't you? I mean you didn't say that so I wouldn't think badly of you, did you?"

"No, I wouldn't lie to you." The time she had dreaded for a long while had finally arrived.

"Then tell me the whole story and not just the parts you used to think I'd understand without asking too many questions," he persisted. "You used to tell me I'd have to wait until I was older. I think I've finally reached that point," he grumbled.

Sara stifled her smile. For a boy who would be ready to shave soon, he appeared the picture of youth.

"I don't think you have too much to worry about growing too old too fast," she said drily. "But you're right, it is time for you to hear the entire story." She stared down at the clasped hands, needing those moments to gather her thoughts, unsure where to begin her story, because there were some things she could not reveal.

"You met in college," Tim prompted.

Sara nodded. "Your father had the same rebellious streak you now show, and he was very stubborn, just as you are." She pictured the lanky young man always dressed in faded jeans, T-shirt and a beat-up denim jacket. "There really isn't a lot to say, and it's an old story you see on the late show every so often. After awhile I wanted to get married, he thought we were too young, and now that I'm older and, hopefully, wiser, I agree with him, but at that time I was positive I knew better, because I pressed for a commitment he couldn't give me." She smiled sadly. "We argued, I felt he didn't love me as much as I loved him, so I left."

"He didn't know you were pregnant?"

She shook her head. "I didn't know I was until I had been back here a couple of months."

"But you didn't call him." He spoke it as a statement instead of a question.

"No, I didn't," she murmured. "Tim, by now you should know I have a great deal of pride. Much more than one person needs, which unfortunately you inherited. Since he didn't try to contact me I wasn't going to contact him if I could help it. I forgot that we never really talked all that much about our pasts, and he never learned what town I was from. I decided it was best I go on with my life and not worry about something that couldn't be easily taken care of. I did break down and tried to call him after you were born, because I wanted him to know he had a son, but his number had been disconnected, and when I tried to call his friends, no one knew where he was." Where had he gone then? she still wondered. A few times that thought cropped up, but it always disappeared as quickly as it appeared.

Tim's face was set in bitter lines too old for his young age. "He just didn't give a damn about us, did he? Otherwise he would have tried to find us," he pronounced.

She shook her head, remembering the pain in Jess's eyes when he'd first confronted her with his newfound knowledge. "No, there was no way for him to find us." She grasped his hands tightly when he tried to pull away. "Don't hate the man for something that was beyond his control," she urged. "Tim, hate is a disease that will eat you up and leave you with nothing."

"But it's because of him people treat you the way they do," he argued vehemently, his fishing pole all but forgotten.

"No, it isn't. I could have gone anywhere and said I was a widow or divorced and no one would have been the wiser. I know this has been hard for you, and I'm sorry for that, because I never wanted you to be hurt."

Tim winced, thinking of the times he'd hurt his mother with his thoughtless behavior and silently vowed to do better in the future. He didn't voice his vow out loud in case he wasn't able to keep it as strongly as he might like to.

"You know," he said finally, "maybe we should have done this before."

"The last person you've wanted to be with during the past few years is your mother," Sara teased.

Tim grimaced. "Yeah, well, I've got an image to maintain, you know."

She laughed, relieved he hadn't asked further revealing questions, because she didn't feel comfortable telling all just yet, because frankly she didn't know how to tell him his father was now living in their town. That particular truth would have to come out eventually, just not yet.

The few hours Sara and Tim spent together that morning were the beginning of subtle changes in their lives. Sara noticed Tim didn't go out as much, and he even began studying more. He also made himself available at the gas station several afternoons a week. Sara silently rejoiced in this new side to her son even as she pragmatically didn't expect it to last forever. Tim was too much a free spirit for that.

She also couldn't get away from thoughts of Jess no matter how hard she tried. A day didn't go by when someone didn't make a comment about him to her.

"Such a nice young man," Lila Thornton enthused when she picked up her car after having it tuned up. "Do you know he spent well over an hour with Daddy yesterday?" It was a well-known fact that Lila's father was an irascible old man who would try the patience of the most revered saint. Sara hid her smile at the thought of Jess listening to Toby Thornton's stories about the war. The elderly man must have been overjoyed to have a new listener.

Caroline Morgan told Sara how much Reverend Larkin complimented her on her pecan pie and ate two pieces.

Leona Matthews told her how that new preacher carried her groceries home one afternoon when she discovered her car had a dead battery.

"Doesn't he ever screw up?" Jackson grumbled, one afternoon.

"Who?" Sara asked absently sitting back in her chair, the two front legs tilted upward.

"That new preacher, that's who. You always said he was a regular hellion. The way people talk you'd think he was buckin' for a first-class room in heaven."

"That's something you won't have to worry about," she murmured, hiding her smile. "I'm sure your room will be situated a great deal farther south."

The elderly man glared at her. "You're really full of it lately, and I bet he's got somethin' to do with it."

"I do have to admit Tim's improved nature has also improved mine," Sara told him serenely.

"That's not what I meant, and you know it," Jackson grumbled. "I saw your face sorta light up when that preacher came in for gas yesterday. You acted like some high-school girl around the football captain." He snorted with disgust.

Sara hated herself for the blush that crept into her cheeks. "That preacher has a name," she reminded him.

"I ain't so feeble I forget someone's name." He turned back to his work.

That was true, she agreed privately. Jackson's selective memory was probably the best in the county, if not the state.

"I'm going up to the house to fix lunch," she announced, standing up and walking up the brick-lined path.

"No beans," he shouted after her. "They give me indigestion."

"As if I'd forget."

TIM FINALLY DECIDED he was in love for the first time in his life.

"Forget it, man," Syd, one of his friends, advised during lunch one day after seeing Tim stare at Lora for the past fifteen minutes instead of wolfing down his lunch as usual. "She's old lady Masterson's granddaughter, and you know what a snob she is."

"Lora's not a snob," he argued, not taking his eyes off the smiling girl talking animatedly to a group of girls.

"As long as we peasants stay in our section she isn't. If we step out of line though, Chad would take us apart. He's the kind of guy she wants, not someone like us."

"Don't be more of an ass than you are, Syd," he said sharply, grabbing his books as he stood up and walked away, making sure to casually saunter past Lora's table. He happily noticed that she looked up and flashed that million-dollar smile at him before turning back to her friends. For the rest of the day Tim floated through his classes and dreamed of a brown-haired girl with a beautiful smile. He was grinning idiotically when he finally arrived home more than two hours late.

"Where have you been?" Sara demanded, greeting him at the door. "Tim, you promised you'd be home right after school to help us at the station." She spun around staring after him as he waltzed past her without saying a word. "Timothy Murdock, I'm talking to you!"

"Yeah." He sounded distracted.

"What in the world?" Sara watched her son walk into the kitchen, open the refrigerator door, pick up the milk carton, stare at it for a full minute and return it to the refrigerator.

"I'd say the boy is in love," Jackson observed, walking up behind her.

Sara turned her head, looking the picture of dismay. "He's too young!" she wailed, still remembering how he looked in diapers.

Jackson stared at her long and hard. "How old were you when you first fell in love?"

"Oh."

"Yeah, 'oh.' I'd say some pretty li'l thing has caught his eye and turned his brain to pure oatmeal. He's not going to be worth a damn around here until he gets it out of his system."

"He wasn't all that much help before then," Sara muttered, then raised her voice. "Tim, I want to speak to you now."

The boy stood in the doorway of the kitchen. "You wanted me, Mom?"

"No, I was practically screaming your name so I wouldn't forget it," she said sarcastically. "You said you would help out this afternoon, but you never showed up or called." She stopped, realizing he hadn't heard one word.

"Gee, Mom, for a woman your age you've got a pretty good figure," Tim replied dreamily.

"Thanks, I think." Sara looked uncertain at this even more abrupt switch in her son's personality.

"Who's the girl?" Jackson boomed.

"Lora Summers." He made her name sound like a prayer.

"Cora Masterson's granddaughter?" Jackson clarified.

"Yeah."

Sara felt her nerves tighten in reaction. She was already fearing the worst.

"Is she in any of your classes?"

Tim nodded. "History and English. She gets straight A's. She's got a really pretty smile."

"And prune-face Cora for a grandmother," Jackson muttered, subsiding when Sara glared at him.

"Can I trust you to go down to the station and do some work?" Sara asked her son.

He nodded, ambling out of the house.

"I better get out there, too, otherwise he just might decide to give someone regular gas when they need unleaded and still not be able to figure out why the nozzle won't fit," Jackson said, leaving Sara to sort out her fears.

While fixing dinner, she thought over this new turn in Tim's life.

Hadn't he learned in the past that some people refused to allow him to forget his lack of a father? Cora Masterson was one of them. As leader of the town's old guard, the elderly woman felt it was her right to dictate the social mores of the town. So what if those mores had changed over the past forty years. Cora certainly hadn't.

Sara clenched her jaw. She would do anything to spare Tim further pain, and she was afraid he was heading for a major fall if he decided to push his luck with Lora Summers, since it was well known Cora ruled her daughter and son-in-law with the same iron hand she had used with her husband. Sara was surprised they had decided to come back to town.

At first Sara thought seriously about having a long talk with Tim in hopes of dissuading him from further thoughts of Lora, but she knew better. She knew that was the best way to push him away. Besides, the last thing she wanted to do was alienate him after the slow but steady progress they'd made recently.

This was one of those times Sara wished desperately for a father Tim could talk to. Of course, then the problem would be entirely different. For one brief, crazy moment she thought about sending Tim over to Jess. Surely by now Jess realized how narrow-minded a certain faction of the town's population was.

She chopped the vegetables with a vengeance. She was tired of keeping secrets and wondering how long it would be before it all blew up in their faces. Perhaps she should sell the station and move to another town before it was too late.

There was only one problem with that kind of thinking. It was already too late.

WITH EACH PASSING DAY, Sara's frayed nerves unraveled a bit more. She watched Tim moon around the house, and for the first time his appetite was just about nonexistent.

What didn't help Sara's peace of mind were Albert's almost daily visits to the station with one excuse after another—his tires needed air, he thought his radiator was leaking. Each time he asked Sara out, and each time she flatly refused him.

"The day's gonna come when you won't be so choosy, Sara, and you'll be glad to have a man interested in you," he told her one afternoon when he'd stopped by to fill his gas tank.

"I'll worry about that when a real man comes along," she threw over her shoulder as she walked away.

Albert's face turned a bright red. "You bitch," he snarled, walking swiftly after her and grabbing her shoulders, roughly spinning her around.

"Let me go!" she ordered, pulling away.

"Who the hell do you think you are?" Albert shouted, jabbing her in the chest with his forefinger. "You think just anyone wants you now, baby? You're nothing in town...*nothing*. You stay here year after year hoping the old biddies will accept you. Well, forget it, lady." He made it sound like a dirty word. "If you want to get laid, you better settle for what you can get and be happy with it."

Sara's gaze was pure ice. "Get in your truck and get out of here now. And don't ever come back. If you need gas, you can just travel the twenty miles to Charlotte. Your business is no longer welcome here."

"Don't you act so high and mighty with me," he yelled, grabbing her shoulders and shaking her so hard her head flopped back and forth until she was convinced her neck would snap under the strain. "I know you for what you really are."

Sara swallowed a scream at his rough handling and struggled to free herself. As she stepped back she lost her balance and fell backward. Just as her head hit the concrete and her vision faded to black, she saw Tim attack the older man and heard her son's roar of outrage before she knew nothing at all.

Chapter Five

Sara had never experienced a hangover before, but she was convinced this was what one would feel like. Her entire head ached, even her eyelids hurt as she slowly lifted them to scan her surroundings. She knew she was lying down on an unfamiliar bed and she had a horrible headache, but that didn't tell her what was wrong or where she was. The first thing she saw in the darkened room was a shadowy figure seated in a chair next to her bed.

"Jess," she mumbled, keeping her eyes barely open because it hurt too much. What kind of party had she attended last night?

"I'm here, Sara." His voice was soft, not the strong tones she was used to.

"Had the funniest dream," she laughed, then groaned as pain shot through her head. "What did I do to deserve this? Anyway, I dreamed we had a son, and we had split up, and when I saw you again you were a minister." Her lips curved in a faint smile. "Crazy, huh?" She groped with her hand until he grasped it between his two.

There was a moment of silence before he replied in a quiet voice. "Yeah, crazy. It was probably due to the bump on your head."

"My head hurts," Sara whimpered, moving her head slowly in order to see him better.

"Go back to sleep," he advised. "The next time you wake up you'll feel much better."

"Don't go 'way." Her voice trailed off. "I want to tell you about the rest of my dream."

"I'll be here."

"Promise."

"Promise." Jess sat back in the chair, his leg propped against his knee, his fingertips rubbing his chin reflectively and listening to Sara's breathing deepen as she fell back into a drug-induced sleep.

For a moment he had also drifted back in time just as Sara had. He knew it was her head injury that had scrambled her thoughts, but it didn't stop him from recalling those days . . . and nights.

Sara always had a smile on her face, and without sounding egotistical, Jess knew she had loved him deeply back then, but he also knew he hadn't been ready for such a heavy-duty commitment as marriage would have required. It saddened him that she had borne their child alone and suffered the malice of the townspeople. Yet would things have been any better if he had known about her pregnancy and they had done the right thing by marrying? True, Tim would have carried his name, and he would have had a father, but there was no guarantee they would have stayed married. Would Tim have fared better with what could have been a part-time father or no father at all? Those were questions he had no answers to. He rubbed her limp hand between his two, more for his own comfort than hers.

To his dying day Jess wouldn't forget the sight that greeted him when he drove past the gas station. He pulled in when he saw Albert touching Sara lewdly, her stepping away and falling and an enraged Tim attacking the older man. For a split second Jess's once hairtrigger temper flared up, and he visualized his own hands around Albert's neck. Instead of giving in to old temptations, he stopped his truck and jumped out, pulling Tim off Albert while a loudly swearing Jackson cradled Sara in his arms.

Jess called on all his powers of persuasion with Albert, who was trying to stem the blood that streamed from his nose and threatening to have Tim put in jail. Only Jess's quietly spoken advice that if Tim was jailed, the true reason for the accident would come out silenced him. Then Tim turned on Jess informing him in no uncertain terms that he didn't need any help from a wimpy do-gooder like him. Jess was very tempted to take the boy out back and show him how much a wimp he was, but tamped down the idea before he gave in to a temper that used to be every bit as fierce as Tim's was.

Jess only hoped Tim learned to control the infamous Larkin temper before it got him into deep trouble.

WHEN SARA AGAIN OPENED her eyes she slowly turned her head and found Tess sitting in the chair next to her bed and Tim pacing the floor by the window.

"Tess?" Sara's voice cracked. She ran her tongue over her dry lips.

"Sara, honey, how are you?" Tess leaned forward and poured a glass of water for her. "Do you want me to call the nurse?"

"No, don't call anyone. I know I hit my head, so why does every bone in my body hurt, too?" She managed a feeble smile for her son as he hung over the bed staring at her as if afraid she'd die at any moment. Her expression sobered when she noted the bruise on his cheekbone. "Oh, Tim."

"Don't worry about me, he got it much worse," he assured her in a hard voice reminiscent of his father's.

"Tim, this is no time to upset your mother," Tess spoke up sharply. "Why don't you go out and get a Coke or something? If you need some money, go ahead and get some out of my purse." She leaned forward, supporting Sara's shoulders as she sipped the cool water.

"Thanks." Sara collapsed against the pillows. She waited until Tim had left the room, closing the door behind him. "Tess, do you know if Jess was here? I'm not sure if I dreamed his presence or not, but I could have sworn I woke up before and found him here. I must have been doped up or something, because I thought I was back in college and we were still together."

"He did stay with you for a little while last night," she admitted.

Sara drew in a deep breath. "Was anyone else here? I don't know what I said, if I said anything at all, but if the wrong person overheard..." Her voice trailed off.

"He was alone," Tess assured her. "When Tim and I came in about a half hour ago, Jess was already gone. Tim and Jess rode over here in the ambulance with you yesterday, and I came as soon as Jackson called and told me what happened." Her eyes were dark with concern. "We've all been worried sick about you."

Sara closed her eyes, fighting her headache in vain. "Tess, what exactly happened to me?"

"Honey, I don't know the whole story. All Tim said while you were being treated was that he was going to kill Albert for hurting you."

Sara nodded, then winced as the pain swept through her head again. "Oh, yes," she groaned. "Damn! Can't a person get some aspirin around here? Or have hospitals stopped treating sick people?"

Tess looked guilty as she leaned over to press the call button for the nurse. "We were only allowed to stay in here as long as we promised to call as soon as you woke up."

And Tess was properly chastised when the nurse arrived and ascertained Sara had been awake longer than a minute or so. Tess was shooed outside when the doctor arrived to examine Sara more thoroughly and pronounced her fit enough to go home the next day as long as her headache was gone by then and there were no further complications.

Tess walked out to the lobby and found Tim sitting morosely in a corner chair.

"The doctor's taking a look at her now," she explained, sitting on a nearby couch. "He'll come out to tell us his diagnosis when he's finished."

"I should have killed him," he muttered, a dark scowl marring his face.

"Don't ever say anything like that!" Tess ordered, leaning forward.

"You weren't there, Tess. You didn't see what that bastard did to her," he argued. "He—he touched her!" His face reddened with adolescent embarrassment as he recalled exactly where Albert touched Sara.

Tess could easily guess the rest. "Albert was always a jerk. Besides, you left him with a few painful reminders that I'm sure were difficult for him to explain to his wife. Leave it at that, Tim. Don't hurt your mother more by getting into additional trouble." She smiled. "She needs you a great deal, Tim. You have to be there for her."

Tim studied the woman who had been like a second mother to him and had always been willing to listen when he needed to talk something out that he couldn't talk over with his mother. He'd made use of Tess's more than willing ear several times.

"He's always saying things to Mom, talking about her as if they..." He stopped, unwilling to go on.

Tess sighed, recognizing his distress. "Tim, all of us have known for years what a crass jerk Albert is, and we generally ignore him when he's out pretending to be the town stud. You'll hate me for saying this, but you're still young, and you have a lot to learn about the adult male of the species. I only hope this episode will teach you how *not* to be."

"Tess." Jess stood before them. "Tim, how is your mother doing?" he asked, looking every inch the town preacher in his dark blue suit, white shirt and conservative tie.

Tim shrugged, still feeling remnants of anger at the man who had pulled him away from Albert before he could inflict too much damage. "The doctor's looking at her now," he mumbled sullenly, then yelped, turning to glare at Tess who had pinched him hard.

"She still has a headache, but her color's good, and she's beginning to sound more like herself," she explained, fully prepared to pinch Tim again if he said or did anything rude. That Jess spent a few hours in Sara's room last night had been kept from Tim, because Tess and Jackson knew he wouldn't have understood why the town's new minister would spend so much time with one of his flock. "I have an idea she'll be kept here for another day or so, and even then she's going to have to take it easy for awhile."

"I'll try to stop in and see her before I leave," Jess said smoothly. "Mrs. Lassiter fell and broke her hip a few days ago, and I thought I'd come by and see her now that she's beginning to feel well enough to accept visitors." He looked at Tim. "I see your face doesn't look as frightening today."

"I bet Albert doesn't look so great either." He stood up. "I'm gonna get something to eat." He left them without saying another word.

"What happened?" Tess demanded, once Tim was out of earshot. "Is Albert definitely going to drop the charges?"

Jess nodded. "Deep down the man is a coward when it comes to his wife's temper. Jackson and I assured him the story for public consumption will be that Sara slipped and hit her head and Albert banged up his face while trying to catch her before she fell. I'm sure not everyone will believe the story." He grinned. "Jackson thought it up."

"No wonder. It's full of enough holes," Tess said drily.

"I better get on to Mrs. Lassiter's room." Jess appeared reluctant to move. "Please tell Sara I'll try to stop by and see her later."

Tess stared closely at the dark-haired man finding it difficult to equate this sober creature with the wild and free lover Sara had mentioned. Tess swore she could see traces of that old devilment in his eyes and the cocky stance he must have once exhibited to the world when he had been younger and not so wise.

"Damn, you must have been something sixteen years ago," she murmured, a wry smile touching her lips.

He grinned back with a touch of his old wickedness. "Careful, Mrs. Howard, you're going to ruin my reputation."

"Give me a break. In case you haven't noticed, church attendance has risen sharply in the past few weeks, and most of them are women."

"They'll get the message—one way or another."

Tess shook her head as she stood up. "Then why do I have the feeling things will get worse before they get better?"

Jess laid his hand on her shoulder for a brief moment. "Have faith, Tess," he advised. "It's done me a lot of good in the past."

"DOCTOR, I CAN'T STAY HERE two more days!" Sara protested after listening to the man drone on that he was worried about more than her lingering headache.

"You have no choice, Sara," the soft-spoken man countered. "You're anemic, a good seven pounds underweight, and you're on the point of exhaustion."

By then she had tuned out his rambling discourse. When he finished, she requested two aspirin and told him she would stay one extra day and he would have to be happy with that. She didn't brighten until Tim arrived.

"I'll come see you every day," he promised with the fervency of youth after handing her the vase of flowers Tess had given him the money to buy.

"You have school to attend," Sara reminded him gently.

He snorted. "They won't miss me."

"Yes, they will, and with the semester over soon you can't afford to miss too many days. Do this for me, please?"

Tim stared down at the floor, the tips of his ears a bright red. "Come on, Mom. You almost sound too mushy," he muttered, quickly changing the subject.

Jackson also dropped by to see Sara that evening, but that didn't stop her from looking for another visitor. One she both desired and dreaded to see.

When the hospital quieted down after all the visitors left, Sara felt ready for a long sleep. When she awoke the next morning, she was surprised to find a large caramel-colored teddy bear ensconced in the chair beside her bed.

"I see you met your new roommate." The nurse smiled when she entered the room carrying Sara's breakfast tray.

"Who sent him?" Sara asked.

The woman shrugged. "I just came on duty, but there's a card attached." She withdrew a white envelope attached to the large, red bow circling the bear's neck and handed it to Sara, who tore it open, eager to read the name of the sender. She was not disappointed.

I know you're only going to be there one night more, but I thought you might like the company.

Jess

"Enjoy your breakfast." The nurse set the tray down and left the room.

"Oh, I will." She smiled to herself, tucking the note away.

If Sara was disappointed that she didn't hear from Jess again, she didn't admit it, even to herself. She told herself it was for the best. She was still telling herself that when Sunday arrived and she and Tim attended church. Despite what had happened at the hospital— and whatever Sara had mumbled from her hazy half sleep, Jess acted toward her as he would with any member of his congregation. Or so she thought, until Tim challenged that thinking.

"I don't like the way the preacher looks at you," Tim complained as they drove out of the church parking lot.

"What do you mean the way he looks at me?" Sara was surprised by his remark. "He doesn't treat me any differently than he does anyone else."

"Want to bet? The guy is old."

Sara bit her lip to keep from bursting out laughing. She doubted Jess would appreciate being called old when he was only three years older than she was.

"The man is close to my own age," she pointed out.

"Yeah, but you don't act old. Neither does Tess. Now Mrs. Morgan, *she* acts old."

Sara sighed. "Carolyn Morgan is four years younger than I am. I suggest we change the subject before you put both feet in your big mouth and I feel ready for a wheelchair," she said mock sweetly.

Tim frowned, not understanding at first what she meant. Then his brow cleared. "Oh, yeah. Hey, Mom, I told you I don't think you're old. Oh, your hair may be a little gray—" He halted at the set expression on his mother's face. "I should shut up, huh?"

"Bingo," she sang out, then burst out laughing. "Poor Tim, no matter what you say you're going to lose the battle."

"Does this have something to do with what people call the battle of the sexes?"

Sara thought about it. "Yes, I guess in a way it does."
My little boy is growing up so fast, she thought to herself. *So why can't I handle it?* She thought about Jess
and realized she hadn't thanked him for the bear who
now rested majestically on her bed. She promised herself to take care of a thank-you when she got home.

Dear Jess,
Thank you so much for thinking of me while I was
in the hospital. Even after my flowers have gone it's
nice to know my bear will still be here to keep me
company.

                                                    Sara

He crumpled the note in his hand.
"Oh, Sara, would it have hurt so much to call?" he
muttered under his breath.
The old magic was gone. He was intelligent enough
to realize that. Yet there was something there, a faint
trickle of awareness that skittered across his nerves
when he saw her.
He thought about that when he had sat up with her
in the hospital and she had awakened thinking they were
back in school. He knew it was the bump on the head
that had muddled her thinking and even played along
with it so she wouldn't become too agitated. And for a
brief time he had even wished they could have gone
back to those times. Then he sternly reminded himself
that would have been a mistake in many ways. Perhaps
someday he would tell Sara what happened back then
after she left him. It wasn't a pretty story, but one he
knew had to be told.
On the spur of the moment he searched through the
telephone directory and found Sara's home number. He

dialed it, silently praying she would be the one to answer.

"Hello?" His prayer was answered.

"Sara, it's Jess." For a moment he was afraid she had hung up until he heard the soft sounds of her breathing over the phone.

"You shouldn't have called here." Her voice was so soft it was barely a whisper.

"As neither one of us has a party line I don't think there's anything for you to worry about," he told her.

"Why are you calling me?"

"I got your note."

"Don't tell me. You're calling to thank me for the thank-you note." Her tone was sardonic.

"That would be novel, wouldn't it?" Jess said lightly, then rushed on before she could form an excuse to hang up. "Sara, I'm driving into Charlotte Friday on business. I'd like it if you could meet me for lunch or dinner."

He could practically hear her feelings of panic race across the line.

"No," she replied without hesitation.

"Why not?"

"You know very well why not."

"Then humor me."

Sara exhaled a tiny breath. This was the Jess she once knew. "You have an image to maintain in this town. Being seen with me would ruin it."

"Don't you think that should be my worry?" Jess asked gently. "There's no harm in two old friends getting together and talking over old times, is there?"

"There is when the two people are us." Sara fought hard not to give in to him. "Please, Jess, there isn't any reason for us to see each other on a social basis."

"Not even if I want to see you?"

"It wouldn't be a good idea. Jess, I have to go."

"I'll be at the Lamplighter Inn at eleven-thirty and again at seven," he said hastily. "Sara, please come." He hung up before she could offer any further arguments.

Jess leaned back in his chair, wondering why he had pressed Sara so hard. His suggestion that they meet had been made on pure impulse. He hadn't meant to do that. His reason for calling her had been the desire to hear her voice. But after hearing it he wanted more, he wanted to see her without the sharp eyes of the town upon them. He didn't want to see her hurt more than she had been in the past. He had told her the truth; he did have business in Charlotte on Friday. He honestly didn't know if Sara would meet him, but he could always hope.

"WOMAN, I ASKED YOU for that wrench five minutes ago!" Jackson shouted across the garage. "Where is your brain this morning?"

Sara snapped to attention as she guiltily tore her eyes from the round-faced clock hanging on the wall. Eleven-fifteen, Friday morning. She had determinedly ignored that same clock all morning until Jackson had asked her the time forty minutes ago. After that she glanced up almost every five minutes, well aware Jess would soon arrive at the restaurant and would wait for someone who would never appear.

"'Bout time you heard me," Jackson grumbled when Sara finally handed him the wrench.

"I, ah, I thought maybe I'd drive into Charlotte this afternoon and do some window-shopping," she said with what she thought was the right casual touch after they had finished their lunch.

He shot her a narrow-eyed glance. "That might be a good idea," he said finally. "Your brain sure ain't been here all morning."

"Tim will be here after school," she reminded him, now feeling guilty at the idea of taking an afternoon off, although she couldn't remember the last time she had ever taken time off just for herself.

"Go," he ordered. "You don't get out all that much, and it will do you good."

Sara left for the house. In record time she showered and changed into an off-white and blue-striped chambray blouse and blue full skirt with a lace edge around the hem. She pulled her hair back in a French braid and hurriedly used eye shadow, mascara and lipstick.

She looked at herself in the mirror and felt an insane urge to giggle. After spraying on a light floral cologne, she ran out of the house to her car. She would have time to do the window-shopping she'd said she was doing before arriving at the Lamplighter Inn that evening.

TIM WATCHED LORA with what could only be called the hungry eyes of youth as she piled her books together when the bell rang signifying the end of class. He couldn't imagine a more beautiful girl. He rose hurriedly from his chair so he would leave the room the same time as she did.

"Hi, Lora." He affected a cocky grin he'd seen Stallone use in one of his movies, and it worked for him.

"Hi, Tim." She flashed the smile that had won her the position of head cheerleader for the junior varsity. She stopped just outside the classroom and looked up with a coy smile. "I'm having some friends over to-night. Maybe I'll see you there."

It took every ounce of self-control for Tim not to break out in a rebel yell. Instead he looked as if the most popular girl in school invited him over to her house all the time.

"Yeah, maybe."

Lora continued to smile as she walked away, joined by several of her friends.

"I smell trouble, man," Syd told him, coming up from behind.

"You're just jealous, because she didn't ask you," Tim jeered, spinning the knob of his combination lock and opening his locker door.

"Give me a break. Tim, she likes guys who have status, and yours is a complete zero."

Tim grabbed him by the shoulders and slammed him against the lockers.

"You're not funny," he said between gritted teeth, releasing him. Slamming his locker door, he walked away ignoring his friend's entreaties to wait up. In the end Syd walked away in disgust, muttering that Tim would learn the hard way about girls like Lora.

Chapter Six

Sara discovered how to have fun playing hooky for the afternoon. She checked out the new fashions in the stores, bought Tim some jeans and shirts and tobacco for Jackson. As for herself, she indulged in a double scoop of chocolate-chocolate-chip ice cream. As the time grew closer to seven o'clock, she grew more nervous.

How did one act on a date with a minister? She tried to remind herself that this was Jess, the man she had once loved so deeply, the father of her son, except it didn't work. Try as she might she couldn't reconcile the two.

She parked in the restaurant's parking lot a few minutes after seven. The first thing she saw was Jess's Bronco, parked near the entrance. She took the time to freshen her cologne and apply fresh lipstick before getting out of her car and walking slowly to the door.

She spied Jess the moment she stepped inside. As if sensing her presence he stood up, turned around and flashed a broad smile.

"You did come." There was no smug conquest in his voice or in his expression, only pure pleasure at seeing her as he took her hands in his. Without allowing her to say a word he led her toward the hostess, and they were immediately seated in a corner booth.

"I almost didn't come," Sara blurted out once they were left alone.

"But you did." His dark eyes twinkled. He made no move to touch her again, but she experienced the strangest feeling, as if his warmth surrounded her. "And I'm very glad you accepted my invitation." He looked up when the waitress stopped by their table asking if they wanted a drink. He glanced at Sara, who shook her head, then told the waitress the same.

To hide her nervousness, Sara opened the menu and studied the contents.

"Everything looks so good." Was her voice more high-pitched than normal? She silently ordered herself to relax, but it was easier said than done.

"Then you've never been here before?"

"No, I haven't." She continued scanning the menu. "I think I'll have the prawns and a salad."

Jess ordered their meal before turning his attention back to her. "You don't have to be nervous, you know," he teased. "I don't bite."

She lowered her face. "Jess, why are we here?" she asked in a soft voice.

"To have dinner." He looked up and smiled at the waitress as she deposited their appetizers, potato skins and fried zucchini and glasses of iced tea on the table.

"Don't play games with me, Jess," she said in a harsh whisper. "I'm long past that stage with you."

He smiled, a sad sweet smile. "Yes, I guess we are. When I called you, I hadn't intended to ask you out; it just sort of popped out."

His admission surprised her. The Jess she remembered wouldn't have admitted to any kind of vulnerability.

"And I didn't intend to come, so I guess we're even." All her earlier uneasiness had vanished, and her smile was now natural and relaxed as she helped herself to two potato skins and zucchini. "So, what have you been doing the past fifteen years?"

"Straightening out my life, going back to school and preaching," he said glibly.

"Why the ministry?" Sara asked curiously. "Of all the occupations I could picture you in, that isn't one of them."

He looked pensive. "Yes, I'm sure this is quite a switch from the old Jess you knew. It's a very long and complicated story and not something to be told over a nice dinner. Why don't we leave it for another day? Instead I'll tell you how lovely you look tonight."

"Thank you for the compliment, even if you only said it in hopes I would change the subject. I won't, you know. I do want to find out why," she told him. "I will promise not to pry too much, though. Will you tell me something about your work before you came to Henderson, or is that another long and complicated story?"

He smiled and shook his head. "No, but it can be pretty boring."

Sara stared long and deep into Jess's dark eyes. "I wouldn't be bored."

"All right, you're asking for it." He then launched into a lengthy discourse on his work with runaways while he lived in Atlanta. He responded to Sara's questions, barely stopping for breath when their meals arrived.

"Why would you want to leave such a fulfilling position to come out here and preach in a small town?" she asked.

Jess's eyes darkened with pain. "I began getting too emotionally involved with the boys' problems," he murmured, toying with the rest of his steak.

"And now you have Mrs. Masterson to contend with. I think you got a raw deal."

Jess's lips twitched. "Yes, she is a bit overpowering at times."

Sara laughed. "Overpowering? Margaret Hamilton could have taken lessons from her on how to properly act like the Wicked Witch of the West."

"She's also the church's main contributor."

"Only because she feels it will put her in charge, just as she's in charge of practically everything else in town."

"But not you."

"But not me," she confirmed. "I'm certain I'm a very nasty spot in her record book, too. I'm sure you've heard all the lurid stories about me."

"Enough." He shook his head, saddened that rumors could be so vindictive. "Why did you stay in Henderson when a fair portion of the townspeople resent you?"

"Because it's the town I grew up in, the school system is good, and I didn't want to hide away for the rest of my life fearing I'd run into someone I knew and perhaps reveal that I wasn't a divorcée or widow after all," she replied candidly. "I didn't want Tim to grow up ashamed that he didn't have a father." Her expression turned bitter, but it was not directed at Jess. "Little did I know that the town that always stood behind its people would shun me. There are so many dark secrets in that town that it's laughable. I'm talking about hot and heavy affairs that are handled so very discreetly, drunken husbands who beat their wives on a regular basis, deputy sheriffs who look the other way when the crimes are committed by sons and daughters of prominent citizens. But, you see, my crime was treated differently. Instead of going out of town to have my baby I had him right there, and then refused to put him up for adoption. I kept my shame with me. Oh, yes, I committed the crime of the century in their eyes because I refused to hide my indiscretion. I have a son, and I'm very proud of him, flaws and all. After fifteen years many of them have finally realized I'm not going away, so I'm more or less tolerated."

Jess felt a pain deep in the region of his heart. He knew Sara didn't blame him for all that had happened, but that didn't stop him from blaming himself for not being more understanding when they'd had their arguments.

He stared down at his plate, his thoughts roaming wild in his head before he looked up. "Sara Murdock, you've grown up into quite a woman."

"If so, you have Tim to thank for doing such a good job of raising me."

"To Tim." Jess raised his glass in a toast.

"To Tim," she echoed, raising her glass.

She couldn't remember enjoying a dinner out more. Jess talked about his hopes and dreams for his new church during the balance of their meal, and Sara talked about the changes she'd made in the station over the past few years during dessert.

"Dinner was wonderful. Thank you." Sara was afraid she sounded all too polite and proper, but she'd finally run out of small talk, and while they had skimmed over what had happened years ago, she had no desire to go into great detail. Why bother rehashing old events that couldn't be changed anyway.

"Thank you for coming." His sincerity was disarming to her. Not that Jess hadn't been sincere before, but now, well, there was a strong peace of mind behind it.

He settled the check, and they walked outside to their cars. He stood by Sara's trusty Mustang as she unlocked the door.

"What's it like to drive an antique?" he teased lightly, leaning against the rear fender.

"I'll have you know this baby is a classic," she informed him, her pert nose turned up daintily in the air. "And between Jackson's and my efforts we keep it in top running condition."

"Aha! A dragster at heart."

"You betcha." Sara laughed, tossing her purse into the passenger seat. Her earlier feelings of unease vanished under his lighthearted manner. "Fred hasn't given up trying to catch me." She mentioned the town's sheriff, who had kept his job more because no one else wanted it than because of his so-called criminal justice skills.

A heavy feeling that had nothing to do with their meal settled in the pit of Jess's stomach as he studied Sara's upturned smiling face. Unthinking, he reached out and cupped her cheek. She froze under his touch, but he wasn't about to allow her to evade him.

"Please, don't Jess," she murmured, a thread of fear in her voice.

"Call it for old time's sake." His head lowered and tilted to one side. His lips barely touched hers once, twice, then retreated in the same slow manner they had captured hers. "See, all very harmless." The streetlight illuminated his slow smile.

Sara's tongue crept out to moisten lips still carrying his taste. "Of course, you were always so right." Her low-voiced reply held a touch of irony. "It was one very harmless kiss that cannot be repeated, ever."

Jess's laugh held disbelief. He stared down into her upturned face fascinated by the way the moonlight caught the blue in her eyes. "You sound as if this were a completely isolated incident that we're to merely tuck away in our book of memories."

"I guess you could say that." She refused to back down now. There was too much at stake here. Jess didn't know the townspeople of Henderson the way she did. And what pain they could bring down on the unsuspecting. She knew even the most innocent of meetings between them could be misconstrued by the wrong people. Tonight was their chance to realize their lives had been meant to part years ago. That she was very sure of. "Our lives are on different levels now, Jess, and they aren't meant to converge. Can't you see that?"

He frowned darkly at her tone of gentle finality. "You sound as if tonight were it, and we'll never see each other again." He didn't like what he was hearing, and he intended her to know it.

"Naturally we'll see each other on Sunday morning. After all, I was baptized in that church, and I don't intend to change now." Sara spoke matter-of-factly, although her insides were churning. She mentally crossed her fingers, praying Jess couldn't tell she was lying. Dinner with him had whetted her appetite for more. She wanted to know what prompted his choice of vocation, and a tiny part of her wondered where he had been fifteen years ago when she had forsaken her pride to try to contact him to tell him he had a son. But, if anything, the years had turned her into a very practical woman.

"And I certainly wouldn't snub you if we ran into each other, but believe me this is for the best. After all, you're new in town, and with your position you must maintain an immaculate image. I don't think that could be accomplished very easily if you were connected with me."

Jess's fists bunched at his side. For years he hadn't had any reason to lose his temper, and in the space of a few moments Sara had managed to chip away at that solid wall.

"You're not making much sense," he finally got out between clenched teeth.

"Yes, I am, Jess, and you know it." Sara opened her car door. "The facts are very simple: you're the town's minister, and I'm their scarlet woman, and never the twain shall meet." She slipped inside and started up the engine, driving off before Jess could protest her words.

"You're wrong about a lot of things, Sara," he muttered, watching her receding taillights. "And very soon I intend to show you." It was a long time before he turned away to climb into his truck and make his way home.

SARA WAS GLAD for the fairly long drive home, because she sorely needed something to concentrate on so she couldn't think about Jess's kiss. It might not have been the most passionate she had ever received from him or anyone, but it touched her soul all the same. She tried to blame it on the late hours, the meal, her hormones suddenly deciding to go out of whack, anything but the truth. Her interest in Jess Larkin was rapidly renewing, but that had to be stopped before it went too far. The pain that would otherwise come wasn't something she could live through again. She wasn't afraid just for herself but also for Tim. She feared if Tim found out about his father, she would lose him and losing him meant losing everything.

When she stopped her car in the garage, it took her a moment to realize she was home, and she had no idea how she'd gotten there. So much for her intense concentration on the road!

"Where the hell have you been?" Jackson's unexpected roar from behind brought a frightened scream to her lips.

"Don't ever do that again! You just aged me a good ten years I can't afford to lose," she gasped as she climbed out of her car.

"Do you know how long I've been waitin' for you to get home?" he went on, ignoring anything she might have to say.

"I ran into a friend in town, and we had dinner." There, she hadn't lied at all. "I'm sorry if I worried you."

"Then you shoulda called," the old man groused. "Fred called a couple hours ago. He's got Tim."

Sara's blood froze. "Tim's in jail?" she croaked, grasping the door handle as her knees threatened to give out. "What happened?"

"He didn't say, but you better get down there right away."

"Yes, I should." She got back in the car, fumbling in her purse for her keys before she found them in her hand.

"Move over," Jackson ordered gruffly, opening the driver's door. "Last thing you need right now is an accident."

Sara surrendered the keys without any protest. The drive to the sheriff's station may have only taken five minutes, but it could have been five hundred for all she knew.

She couldn't remember the last time she had been in the nondescript building set in the middle of town. Tim had been in trouble before, but Fred had always brought him to the house and talked to her there. This had to be very serious indeed, her troubled heart told her. She shivered, feeling very cold although the night air was very warm.

Fred was sitting behind a battered, gray-painted metal desk, his chair tipped back with his feet propped on the blotter.

"Sara." He nodded at the woman standing in the doorway. He stood up, adjusting his belt over his large belly.

"Where's Tim?" Her lips trembled as her eyes searched the empty waiting area for her son.

"He's fine. I did have to put him in a holding cell though."

Sara closed her eyes, visions of bright lights, rubber hoses and other forms of hideous torture running through her mind.

"Buck up, girl," Jackson said gruffly, gripping her elbow tightly when he saw her face pale.

Fred gestured to a rickety wooden chair next to his desk. "I'm afraid it's more than just a broken window or stealing Mr. Carlson's apples this time, Sara," he said in his slow drawl, after she had been seated with Jackson standing behind her in a protective stance, his hand resting on her shoulder.

"What happened?" she continued, fearing the worst. There had to be a mistake!

"There was a fight at the Summers house tonight. One boy ended up with a broken arm, another's got some pretty sore ribs.'' Sara moaned. ''There's also a matter of Chad Lowell's car sporting a broken windshield, slashed tires and a dented hood.''

Sara breathed deeply to keep the nausea at bay. She could feel nervous sweat trickle down between her breasts and down her sides. More than anything she wanted to sit there and have a good old-fashioned bawling session, but this wasn't the time. She drew down deep inside for hidden reserves of strength.

''Naturally we'll pay for the damages.'' She spoke calmly, which was surprising considering the tension in her body.

''It's more than that. Due to the nature of his crimes there will have to be a hearing, Sara.'' Fred's faded blue eyes showed sympathy for her. He had always believed in the motto Live and Let Live, and had only been hard on Tim in the past in hopes he would learn to stay out of mischief and because Sara Murdock was a nice young woman who didn't deserve any more trouble.

She pressed her fingers against her lips as she realized his meaning. ''Judge Carmody?'' she whispered, feeling dread fill her veins.

He nodded slowly.

The nausea threatened to rise again. ''May I take him home? Do you . . . do you require bail or something?''

''I'll release him into your custody, Sara, because I know you'll make sure he stays in town and out of more trouble,'' he assured her. ''I'll give you a call about the day and time of the hearing.''

By then Sara was completely numb. She remained seated in the shabby old chair while Fred sent a deputy to get Tim. She had no idea what she would say to her son when he arrived. She only knew she had to get out of there before she started screaming. She stared down at the scratched linoleum floor, idly noticing the cracks and scuff marks from the many years of use. What seemed aeons later, large feet shod in beat-up Nikes stood before her. She lifted her head slowly to gaze at her son's subdued and apparently frightened, expression. Sara stood up feeling like a very old woman.

"Mom," Tim began tentatively, holding out his hand.

She held her own hand up indicating silence. "No, not now. I have enough to deal with." She led the way out of the station, certain he would follow her.

Jackson stayed behind a moment to speak to the sheriff.

"Did he start it?" Jackson asked.

The other man shrugged. "According to them he did, but we all know what some of those kids are like. I'd say there was a nasty practical joke involved. We just can't prove it. Don't let that boy lose his temper again. Old Man Carmody's going to be tough on him as it is."

Jackson nodded and hurried outside, where Sara and Tim waited in silence by the car.

The silence remained thick during the drive home. When they stepped inside the house, Sara turned to Tim.

"You will not leave this house until further notice," she ordered quietly, her face pale and drawn from the strain.

"Aren't you even going to listen to my side of the story?" he demanded.

"Right now I don't care to listen to anything. I've had it, Tim. You get into trouble at the drop of a hat and try to blame it on everyone else, but this time there's no one else around to blame. Right now I intend to go to bed and I suggest you do the same." Without looking at him, she went into her bedroom and closed the door. It wasn't until she was alone she collapsed on the bed and gave in to tears. The fact that they were for the father and the son made them all the more bitter.

TIM COULDN'T SLEEP due to the anger still nesting in his heart. Anger at kids who thought cruel jokes were funny and anger at a stone-faced mother who refused to listen to him. He lay, still dressed, on his bed in the dark as he thought back over the evening. How could he have been so stupid as to think Lora wanted him to come to her house?

Male adolescent pride was extremely fragile, and Tim's, right now, was shattered into many small pieces. And one very lovely girl with an obvious heart of stone was the cause of it. The events of the evening were going to stay with him for a long time.

Why had she done it?

He had been eager the first part of the evening. Since his mother was gone, he'd only told Jackson he was going to a friend's house and promised not to be out too late.

Lora's parents' house was on the other side of town, a not-too-subtle sign he should have recognized. The two-story white house with bright green trim had been ablaze with lights and sounds of Whitney Houston filtering through the front door. Tim parked his motorcycle out front behind Chad's car, a sleek black Toyota, a present from his father when he made the varsity football team that year. Tim had wryly wondered what he'd get when he graduated the following year.

Tim made a quick check that there were no spots on his shirt or jeans, then ambled up to the door and pushed the doorbell. A giggling Lora opened the door. Upon seeing her visitor, she sobered.

"Tim, what are you doing here?" Her look of curious innocence was a work of art.

He felt confused. "What am I—You invited me." He stumbled over his words. He suddenly had a very bad feeling.

She laughed, the sound trickling down his spine like a layer of ice. "Oh, come on, Tim. Why would I invite *you*? I mean it's not as if you're part of our group or something. After all, your mother runs a gas station." She made the words sound obscene, and the eyes he always thought of as soft brown were cold and hard like her grandmother's.

The rage building up inside was hot and swift. "You tease," he sneered.

"Now look here, Tim Murdock." Lora's voice rose shrilly.

"What's wrong, Lora?" Chad appeared, slipping a possessive arm around her waist as he glared at Tim. "Aren't you on the wrong side of town, Murdock? Why don't you go back where you belong and leave us good folks alone?"

By then Tim was aware of nothing but the need to hurt someone as badly as he hurt. By the time the sheriff arrived, a couple of Chad's friends were screaming in a combination of pain and outrage, and he stood on the sidewalk holding a wrench over the shattered windshield of Chad's car while Chad screamed obscenities at him. While the sheriff led Tim away, he heard the group swear he'd be in jail until he was an old man if they had anything to do about it.

From there it was listening to Sheriff Travis ask him what had happened, and he merely shook his head for an answer. In the end the man sighed and led Tim downstairs to one of the two holding cells to wait for his mother. The other cell housed Otto, who was affectionately known as the town drunk. Tim sat on the hard cot, inhaling the sharp tang of disinfectant as he waited, God knew how long, for his mother to come get him.

And now he sat alone in the dark, the anger finally draining away leaving him empty in mind and spirit.

Chapter Seven

Having slept little during the night, Sara was up at dawn. She made a pot of coffee and sat at the kitchen table drinking cup after cup of the strong dark brew.

"You keep that up, and I'll have to pry you off the ceiling before the morning is over," Jackson predicted, shuffling into the kitchen, pouring himself the last of the pot and taking the time to fix a fresh pot before sitting down.

"As long as I feel nothing, I'll be happy," she murmured, staring into her cup as if it held all the answers to her problems.

"This is the first time Tim's done anything really serious, Sara. The judge will take it into account," Jackson assured her gruffly. "You don't have to worry."

She shook her head. "You forget he'll be seeing Judge Carmody, who believes anyone remotely resembling a juvenile delinquent should be locked away until he's ninety." She choked back a sob. Funny, she thought she was all out of tears. She looked over at him with fear clouding her eyes. Fear of what this hearing could bring.

"Jackson, what am I going to do?" she cried.

Unable to give her an answer he could only sit there and pat her hand, giving her what meager comfort he could.

An hour later Jackson announced he'd open the station and advised Sara to take it easy that morning. There hadn't been a sound from Tim's room.

She showered and dressed in dark blue twill pants and a pink and blue print blouse. After a light application of makeup and piling her hair up on top of her head she felt a bit more normal. Sara knew what she had to do, and she also knew she would have to wait until a more respectable hour to do it. She was in the midst of loading the washer when Tim appeared, looking as sick as she felt.

"I guess saying I'm sorry won't help much, huh?" he muttered, pulling the milk carton out of the refrigerator.

Sara finished loading the washer and turned it on. "It would be a beginning," she said quietly. "Why did you do it, Tim?"

He shrugged, trying to look his usual cocky self. "Seemed like a good idea at the time."

"Don't give me that!" she snapped. "Do you realize how much trouble you're in? Tim, you could very well be sent away." Her voice broke at the thought. "I need to know exactly what happened."

"Why? You didn't care to hear about it last night," he said sullenly.

"Last night I was in shock at coming home to find my son in jail. Today I want to hear what happened. And I want the truth, because that will be the only way I can help you."

"Help me? Come on, Mom. We already know what's gonna happen." He looked grim and frightened at what could happen to him. He wished he had thought about that before he had lost his temper.

"Dammit, tell me!"

Tim related the story in a monotone, keeping his eyes on Sara's face the entire time. When he finished, he breathed a sigh of relief to see she believed him.

"There's nothing we can do, Mom," he admitted on a hollow note.

She remained silent, drumming her fingers on the tabletop. "There might be a way," she said finally.

"What?"

She shook her head. "There's no guarantee, but if I accomplish this, you'll have to swear to me you'll go along with whatever happens, because it may be the only way I can keep you out of jail."

Tim agreed reluctantly. Sara felt ill inside, because she knew there was only one person who could help them, and she would have to swallow a mountain of pride to obtain that help. For her son she would do it and more.

After breakfast Sara wrote out a list of chores for Tim to do and ordered him to be busy working on them while she was gone. Ten minutes later she parked her car in front of a one-story, white clapboard house with brightly colored flowers flanking the porch. For a moment she hesitated, her foot hovering above the bottom step. Then gathering up her courage, she ran up the five steps and rang the doorbell before she lost her nerve. Mrs. Harris, who had been the housekeeper for Reverend Mapes for more than thirty years and now worked for Jess, appeared.

"Yes?" Sara couldn't help but wonder if the gray-haired woman ever smiled.

"Good morning, Mrs. Harris," she greeted the older woman pleasantly. "Is Pastor Larkin in?"

Mrs. Harris eyed her as if she wore a black leather miniskirt and skimpy top instead of her sedate skirt and blouse. "He's busy working on his sermon and doesn't like to be disturbed." She remained behind the safety of the closed screen door.

Sara tamped down her impatience. "Would you please ask him if he could give me a few minutes?"

She debated, then turned away muttering, "I'll see." Within a minute she returned to the door with a startled expression on her face. "He said he'd see you. Mind you, don't keep him long."

Sara nodded as she walked down the hallway to the addition that housed the minister's office. The door stood open with Jess standing under the arch.

"Good morning, Sara. You're out early today." Dressed in faded jeans and a white cotton shirt with the cuffs rolled back, he looked more like the Jess she remembered. "Please, come in. Would you like some coffee?"

"No, thank you," she murmured, suddenly uncomfortable with her reason for being here.

Jess closed the door and returned to his desk. He couldn't help but notice the lines of strain around her mouth and the purple shadows under eyes reddened from crying. Where was the smiling, relaxed woman he had seen twelve hours ago? He leaned back in his chair, his fingers laced across his flat stomach as he waited for Sara to tell him her reason for being here.

"I realize it's crazy for me to be here after my high-minded speech last night," Sara blurted out. "But I don't know where else to go, and this is something you have experience in."

"What can I do to help?"

She almost broke down after his quiet statement. "It's Tim." She quickly related the events of the previous night.

"But if this is his first serious offense, he'll probably get off with a warning and the requirement he has to pay for the damage he caused," Jess assured her.

Sara shook her head. "You don't know Judge Carmody. He makes Judge Roy Bean look like a cream puff. This man believes the best way to handle juveniles is to hand out stiff sentences the first time around so they won't be tempted to stray again. And if they do, then they weren't good kids to begin with. He's known for saying what a shame it is that paddling was outlawed. What Tim did was serious, yes, but sending him away won't accomplish anything except turning him into a very bitter boy."

She stared down at her hands, which nervously twisted her purse strap. "I don't know what to do, Jess," she confessed wearily. "I'm so afraid the worst will happen."

He didn't speak for a few moments. "Is he truly sorry for what he did?"

She nodded, saying wryly, "He has your temper, but is very quick to cool off afterward."

A smile twitched the corners of his lips. "Ah, yes, the infamous Larkin temper," he mused. "Didn't he inherit any of my good points?"

"He's always there for the underdog."

Jess closed his eyes to hide the pain he felt. What had Sara gone through all those years coping with a boy who was quick to fly off the handle? For some divine reason they had been meant to part at that crucial time in their lives and to go on to new experiences that had shaped their characters. No longer was Sara the somewhat flighty young woman. She had grown into a mature, self-assured woman who had had to learn to roll with the punches the hard way. And he certainly didn't go hunting for a fight anymore when things didn't go his way.

"Sara, I cannot honestly go before a judge and vouch for Tim's character when I don't know him all that well." He broke the news to her gently since it hurt him just as much as it hurt her. No, Tim didn't belong in jail. And if anyone knew that, it was himself.

Her lips trembled as she strove to keep her composure. "I—I realize you can't lie, but surely you can think of something that would help him." She held her hands out. "Please, Jess. I'm so frightened over the outcome."

He stood up and walked around his desk to lean against the polished wood. He grasped her hands, rubbing his thumbs over her knuckles.

"I do have an idea," Jess mused. "But it's a gamble."

Sara looked up at him, but her head had trouble cooperating when her senses were painfully aware of the warmth of his hands covering hers and his lean figure standing before her.

"Don't," he whispered, his voice harsh.

"Don't what?"

He dropped his hands and turned away, jamming his hands into his back pockets. "You were the one who coolly stated we were better off not seeing each other on a social basis," he said roughly, refusing to turn back around. "I didn't like it, but I was prepared to accept your edict, because I understood why. If necessary, I would have even found a new church." He drew in a deep breath. "But you make it difficult to keep to those rules when you show up barely twelve hours later asking for my help." He spun around, revealing pain etched in his features.

"I had to come to you," Sara murmured, damping down a desire she knew she couldn't afford to feel. There were too many differences in their lives now to even contemplate it. "I've been up most of the night racking my brain for a solution, but nothing could come to mind." Tears shimmered in her eyes. "I'm so tired of fighting alone."

Jess whistled a tuneless melody between his teeth. "Send Tim over after lunch," he ordered. "I'm going to lay down some ground rules for him, and they won't be easy. If he agrees, then I'll do what I can, but I can't make any guarantees."

"I realize that, and you won't have any problems with him," she said swiftly.

Jess looked skeptical. "I thought you once said he's a lot like me."

"He is."

"Then I hope you have a lot of faith, because you're going to need it."

Sara stood up. "For the longest time I didn't want to believe in anyone." Her smile was misty. "Until now."

Jess had faith, but he also knew problems could crop up if he wasn't careful. He'd worked with a lot of troubled kids over the past ten years. So why did he feel uneasy about this one?

"Jess," Sara said, appearing unsure of herself as she shifted from one foot to the other. "I, ah, I—" she shook her head to clear her thoughts "—I realize I'm pretty gutsy to see you after my high-handed manner last night, and you had every right to refuse my request. Thank you."

He held up his hand to silence her. "Sara, I understand why you said what you did last night, and I also understand why you came today. After all, I am your minister. Why don't we just see what happens? Okay?"

"You mean what hand fate deals us?" she asked wryly.

The corners of his lips moved upward. "More like the hand God deals us," he corrected gently.

"Yeah." She had the grace to look abashed. "I tend to forget you're not the Jess I once knew." She slipped out of the room before he could reply.

Jess returned to his desk, but couldn't resume work on his sermon. Not when he wanted to give thanks that Sara had come to him. He still wasn't sure if they had any kind of future together, but he wanted the chance to find out. He wasn't stupid—he knew close association with Sara could prove harmful to them both, not to mention Tim, if the truth of his parentage ever came out at the wrong time. Because he wanted Tim to know he was his father. It may have been too late to become a parent, but he'd like to become his friend.

"Reverend?" Mrs. Harris knocked and poked her head around the open door. "Would you care for some coffee and fresh-baked oatmeal cookies?"

He grinned. "And if I know your cookies, they're chewy with plenty of chocolate chips in them. Mrs. Harris, you're adding another ten pounds to my frame. Pretty soon I'll have to roll down the aisle."

The housekeeper beamed with pleasure. "I just want to make sure you have everything you need." She paused. "Is Miss Murdock all right? I heard her son was in jail last night for badly hurting some boys." The cold disapproval in her voice indicated her feelings toward the Murdock family.

For a moment Jess was sorely tempted to shock the self-righteous woman with a few home truths, but he subsided, fully aware he wasn't supposed to give in to such things.

"I'm sure Ms. Murdock has enough on her plate without having to worry about gossip." His tone was faintly reproving.

She flushed. "I'll get your coffee," she murmured, slipping away.

Jess sighed. The more he heard, the more he realized Sara's fears weren't all of her own making. He had thought that moving to a small town would give him the rest he needed from the pressures of the halfway house he'd worked in. Instead he had walked into another Peyton Place, where he was one of the characters needed to fill out the cast. He could see the story line now.

Rebellious youth turned preacher arrives in small town where former lover resides with their love child and lives stoically under a cloud of malicious gossip. Oh, yes, this was the stuff soap operas were made of. No wonder they say truth is stranger than fiction.

"NO WAY!" TIM SHOUTED, his hand slicing through the air. "You're not getting me near that holy house. I won't do it."

"You have to," Sara argued. "It could be your only chance to stay out of jail."

"Old Man Carmody wouldn't dare send me to jail," he blustered, but the fear in his eyes belied his brave talk. He'd heard talk about the narrow-minded judge who didn't believe in the old phrase Boys will be Boys. "Besides, who says that do-gooder can do anything? Just 'cause he says so? Give me a break," he scoffed.

Because he's your father, she wanted to scream at him, but she kept her mouth shut. This was definitely not the time. Not when she needed Tim's full cooperation.

Sara did something she had never done in her life. She poured herself a cup of coffee and added a generous portion of whiskey to it. She hated herself for this display of weakness, but she was at her wit's end.

"Mom." Tim was horrified to see her take a drink. Liquor was something she almost never touched, except when she had had that bad toothache one night. Then he saw the tears in her eyes and knew he was the cause. For the tough guy he portrayed to the world, he was a regular marshmallow where she was concerned. "Okay, I'll talk to the guy. But that doesn't mean I'll go along with what he says." He picked up her coffee cup and dumped the contents into the sink. "Larry's mom drinks her coffee like that. You don't want to turn into a turnip brain like her, do you?" he said gruffly.

Sara ducked her face to hide her expression of pleasure. Tim tried so hard to keep his good traits under wraps. She was glad he didn't try hard enough.

"You can go over there around one o'clock," she told him, as he poured her a fresh cup of coffee and set it before her.

"He'll probably make me memorize the whole Bible," he muttered, walking out of the kitchen. "Isn't it enough I go to church every week?"

"And most times you sleep through the sermon," Sara called after him.

"Hey, Reverend Mapes was an all-right guy, but you have to admit he was pretty boring sometimes. Can you imagine being a preacher's kid? You couldn't have any

fun at all. Mom, you okay?'' He ran back to clap her on
the back as she choked on her coffee.

"Yes, I'm fine." She breathed deeply. "Why don't
you help Jackson until lunchtime? Then you can take a
shower and change your clothes before going over to
Pastor Larkin's."

"A shower and clean clothes, too? God, Mom, what
I do for you." He shook his head as he left the house.
"I still think we'd be all right without anyone's help"
were his parting words.

"Not anymore, my love," Sara murmured. "Not
anymore."

TIM STILL FELT SKEPTICAL about this meeting when he
approached the pastor's house. Under orders he had
showered and changed into clean jeans and T-shirt before lunch. He was surprised his mother hadn't in-
spected his ears to make sure they were clean, too, since
this seemed so important to her.

He hadn't missed Mrs. Harris's expression of faint
disgust as she led him through the house to the backyard.

You'd think I was going to steal her blind, he
thought, as she opened the back door and gestured
outside.

"Reverend." The older woman's voice was notice-
ably warmer, but still held a trace of wariness and
something else Tim couldn't identify as she studied him
closely. "The Murdock boy is here."

"Thank you, Mrs. Harris," he called out. "Come on
out, Tim. It's too nice to stay inside."

He ventured outside and found Jess standing near a
large green-and-white metal gardening shed. Wearing
only a pair of faded cutoffs, he looked far from the

picture of the stately minister Tim saw on Sunday mornings.

"Hi, Tim." Jess greeted him with a broad grin. "Why do I have the idea your mother made you clean up before she allowed you out of the house?" His own brief clothing showed smudges of dirt, and his bare body gleamed with sweat.

"I think it's part of a contract they sign when their babies are born," Tim muttered, looking as if he wished he were anywhere else but here. "You know, kids aren't allowed to get dirty, or if they do, no one outside the family can see them that way."

Funny how that phrase about family brought a pang to Jess's heart. He wondered if Tim had been like him as a small child and believed mud was better than any article of clothing. How had Sara dealt with that muddy facet of the Larkin nature years ago?

"I thought we could begin rebuilding the fence at the edge of the property." Jess gestured with the hammer he held in one hand.

Tim looked confused. "Wait a minute. You expect me to work?"

He nodded. "You better take off your T-shirt. You're going to end up pretty dirty." He looked down at his own dirty attire. He gathered up the necessary tools. "You want to grab that box of nails over there?" He walked off expecting Tim to follow.

"Hold on," Tim protested, standing his ground. "Look, I know my mom made some kind of crazy deal with you in hopes of keeping my ass out of jail, but she didn't say anything about my having to work it off. No way, José! You can find yourself another sucker." He stalked off.

"All right, Tim. Then I'm sure you can find a way to keep your ass out of jail." Jess's calm words slowed the boy's escape.

"You shouldn't swear, you know," Tim sneered. "It could ruin your do-good image with your flock."

Jess shrugged. "Naturally there's a good part of that vocabulary I don't use anymore, but sometimes it takes something like that to get a person's attention while others will just settle for a simple show of superior body strength. If you'd feel better, we could arm wrestle. Best two out of three?"

Tim, always known for his glib tongue, didn't know what to say for once. It was clear this man wasn't going to write him off as a lost cause too easily.

"You top me by a good three inches. You'd probably win, even if I am younger."

"The mind has as much to do with winning a contest as does physical strength, so my size has nothing to do with it," Jess pointed out mildly.

"The mind can't beat somebody in arm wrestling," Tim scoffed.

"Wanna bet?" Jess ambled over to the redwood patio table. He sat down, planting his elbow on the table. "Come on, show an old man how it's done." He winced inside. An old man at thirty-nine? Of course, he got out of bed a little slower nowadays, especially after that killer volleyball game where he'd redoubled his efforts in order to show off in front of Sara. He'd paid for it dearly the next day.

Tim hesitated. In the end his pride won the internal battle. He walked slowly over to the table and sat down on the bench across from Jess. He set his elbow on the table, his palm flat against Jess's.

"I don't want to hurt you too much," Tim warned, their fingers curling downward.

"Sounds fair to me," Jess agreed easily. "On the count of three. One, two, three." A light groan left his lips. Tim hesitated a fraction of a second, a fraction too long, and he found his arm flat on the table.

"You cheated!" Tim accused with the dark glare of one who hated being bested by anyone.

"I used my mind, and you fell for it."

Tim's temper began to rise, but he couldn't find an outlet for it.

"I used to have a bad temper, too," Jess told him. "There used to be people who were afraid to talk to me for fear of setting it off."

"You? Come on."

"Me. I used to get into so much trouble my parents were convinced the hospital had switched babies," he confided, man-to-man.

Tim laughed. "Mom once said that about me when I threw a couple pair of greasy overalls in with her white sheets."

Jess tucked that piece of information in the back of his mind.

"So if you once had such a lousy temper, how come you don't have it now?"

"I learned how to control it by thinking with my brain instead of my fists."

Against his will Tim found himself interested. "How can that work?"

And Jess began to tell him.

WHEN TIM ARRIVED HOME more than four hours later, he was filthy from head to toe and looked more relaxed than he had in weeks.

"What on earth did you do over there?" Sara asked, dismay lacing her voice.

"We rebuilt a fence. Oh, Mom, the preacher is coming over for dinner tomorrow after church." Tim breezed through the house. "I was telling him what a good cook you were, and before I knew it he invited himself over for chicken and dumplings."

"How nice," she said faintly. *He's coming over for dinner?*

"You know, Mom—" he ducked his head around the door "—I guess he's not so bad after all. He didn't get mad when I cussed when I hit my thumb with the hammer."

"Why does that not make me feel better?" she said with a sigh, wishing Jess hadn't manipulated a dinner invitation, even though she probably owed him one for what he was doing for her.

"Don't worry, I'll stick around for a while. I want to see if he ever screws up. I guess I better take a shower. I'm pretty dirty." He disappeared.

Sara didn't expect this at all. For Jess to help Tim, yes. For him to sit down with them for Sunday dinner, no. She just hoped she was up to it.

Chapter Eight

Sara sat through the Sunday morning service feeling as if every nerve ending was exposed. It hadn't helped when Tim told her the pastor coming to dinner might not be so bad since Tim should get on his good side anyway and her chicken and dumplings could go a long way toward accomplishing that. So what if she had to swelter in a hot kitchen precooking the chicken?

For a little over an hour she stared at her hymnal, studied the choir's new robes, absently noted the pew's upholstery and spotted a tiny hole, which she didn't help any by poking at it every so often. In fact she looked everywhere but at the minister speaking so earnestly from the pulpit. She saw plenty of men in the congregation wearing dark blue suits, but they weren't the same as the man before her.

She couldn't sit through a meal with him with Tim and Jackson sitting there while she had to make small talk. Oh, yes, this would be a dinner never to be forgotten.

When the congregation rose for the closing hymn so did she, but she could have been singing a nursery rhyme for all she knew. Afterward she filed out with the others.

"I'm looking forward to that fine dinner Tim says you cook, Sara," Jess said warmly, clasping her hands between his for a brief second as they stood in the foyer.

"Yes, well, Tim exaggerates a lot," she said weakly, eager to escape.

Recognizing her distress, he released her instantly and bade her a good day.

"Can I drive?" Tim asked as they approached the car.

"No," she bit out, sliding behind the wheel.

"How am I supposed to get any experience if you won't let me? I could flunk my driving test, because you won't let me practice," he grumbled.

"Don't worry, they'll let you take it until you get it right." She cursed under her breath when the gears protested her abrupt treatment.

"Some example you're setting for me," he said piously, wilting under her fierce glare. He subsided into silence for a few minutes before daring to speak again. "Mom, are you mad because the preacher's coming to dinner?"

"It would have been nice if I had been consulted first."

"But you're always complaining I'm not polite enough, and when he started talking about not gettin' out very much, I thought it was all right to have him over although he invited himself over."

"Having good manners means you ask your mother if it's all right to invite someone over for dinner."

"You've never forgiven me for that," Tim told her with an injured air.

Sara racked her brain for the reason behind his statement. "Something tells me I'm crazy to ask this, but I rarely have sane moments. Exactly what is it I've never

FREE BOOKS & GIFTS CLAIM

Yes, please send me my 4 free Silhouette Desires and my 2 free gifts - and reserve me a special Reader Service subscription. If I decide to subscribe I shall look forward to receiving 6 alluring Silhouette Desires each month for just £7.80 - postage and packaging absolutely free. If I decide not to subscribe, I shall write to you within 10 days. The free books and gifts will be mine to keep in any case.
I understand I am under no obligation whatsoever - I can cancel or suspend my subscription at any time simply by writing to you. I am over 18 years of age.

6S9SD

EXTRA BONUS

This stylish canvas tote bag is yours FREE together with a special mystery gift - when you return this card

Name _____

Address _____

_____

_____ Postcode _____

Signature _____

SEND NO MONEY NOW - TAKE NO RISKS

Reader Service
FREEPOST
PO Box 236
Croydon
Surrey
CR9 9EL

NO STAMP NEEDED

Silhouette Desire

forgiven you for?'' She pulled into the carport and switched off the engine.

"The time I asked Danny, Craig, Lyle and the others over."

"Tim, you asked ten boys over for dinner, a sleep-over and breakfast without asking me first. I believe I had the perfect right to get upset," she informed him, getting out of the car.

"Yeah, but you didn't have to get so bent out of shape," he muttered.

"That episode happened more than five years ago, and if you want to further discuss it, we can talk about what happened to the kitchen when you decided to pop popcorn in the oven at three o'clock in the morning."

"You're right, that happened long ago. Why go over it again?" He slipped out of sight before she could say another word.

"I should have spanked him more when he was lit-tle," she decided out loud, following him into the house, dismally thinking of all the work ahead of her.

"So you're going to let him come here?" Jackson pounced on her the moment she stepped inside.

Sara turned on the old man with a ferocity that took him back a few steps.

"Yes, I'm letting him come here and share a meal with us, and you're going to sit at that table and use the proper table manners your mother once pounded into your thick head. And if you say one word out of line, you'll be eating at Elsie's diner for the rest of your life," Sara threatened darkly.

Jackson shuddered. It was common knowledge that Elsie, the town's spinster, had set her cap for him some forty years ago, and she hadn't given up yet. He refused to set foot inside the diner for fear she'd take it as a favorable sign and send out wedding invitations.

"That's a cruel thing to say, Sara, after all the hard work I've put in here." He adopted his best injured tone.

She flashed him a self-satisfied smirk. "Then I gather we understand each other?"

Still keeping his long face, he ambled out of the kitchen, muttering to himself about the cruelty of women.

"And shave and put on a clean shirt," she called after him.

"Damn women," he spoke under his breath.

"I heard that!"

Knowing she had little time, Sara quickly changed into shorts and T-shirt and proceeded to start dinner. In no time she had the broth simmering and a blueberry cobbler baking in the oven. So they wouldn't have to suffer through their meal in the lingering heat of the kitchen, she instructed Tim to set the dining-room table and switch on the room air conditioner. When she was satisfied everything was under control, she took the time for a quick shower and changed into rose-pink cotton slacks and a striped short-sleeved blouse. That she applied fresh makeup and brushed up her hair was not meant to impress Jess, she told herself as she put away her lipstick and studied herself in the mirror. She really should use eye makeup more often. It did bring out the blue in her eyes. There had once been a time when she wouldn't have left the house without her makeup on. Now she rarely had the time to apply a coat of mascara in the mornings. Rarely took the time was more like it. When she heard the doorbell, she took a deep breath and headed for the front door.

"Reverend," Sara murmured, opening the door and stepping back. Why couldn't he have worn a formal suit and looked all prim and proper instead of wearing pale gray cotton trousers and a gray-and-blue striped shirt with the cuffs folded back and looking absolutely gorgeous?

"Sara." His smile was pure male beauty.

When Sara had first seen Jess again, she had only felt horror that her past had resurfaced and experienced no true feeling for him as a man. It wasn't until she saw him at Tess and Charlie's barbecue that she fully realized the boy had grown up into a good-looking man. Why couldn't he have turned bald and sported a pot belly? Or been married with six kids and had the kind of sweet-faced, sweet-natured wife no one could dislike?

Jess saw the worry in Sara's eyes and understood their meaning.

"I didn't come here to torment you, Sara," he said softly. "I heard chicken and dumplings, and it mushroomed from there."

He stood so close to her she could smell the subtle scent of his cologne. It smelled expensive and sexy. So very like him.

She smiled. "Then I hope you brought your appetite with you, because I usually make more than enough for an army. With the way Tim eats I have to. And don't expect any concessions just because you're company."

He grinned back. "I won't."

To Sara's surprise, dinner turned out to be quite harmless. Jess asked Tim about his interests and learned about his love for his motorcycle. Even Jackson spoke up about his disgust at modern movies—in his opinion there was no one better than Clark Gable and Rita

Hayworth. Not to mention his ideas for pepping up church socials. Sara did suffer a bit when Jackson brought up his idea for a wet T-shirt contest while Tim listened with an eagerness he never displayed for school. She privately decided to have a talk with Jackson later that day. One thing she did enjoy was the sight of father and son talking so easily.

Sara also enjoyed just looking at Jess. He looked so right at her table. When he picked up a piece of chicken and ate it with obvious appreciation, she felt her mouth go dry. She was so lost in gazing at him she hadn't noticed that he was also studying her. She stared across the table at him, seeing something in his eyes she couldn't remember seeing before. And it left her feeling warm.

"Would you care for more salad?" She spoke huskily, feeling the need to break the spell between them and picked up the bowl when he nodded. Sara almost jumped when Jess merely put his hand over hers to steady the bowl while he took what salad he wanted.

"Thank you." He smiled.

She smiled back, unable to think of anything to say and felt a curious sense of relief when all the dinner plates were cleaned.

"Blueberry cobbler anyone?" she asked, wishing her voice would return to normal.

"With French vanilla ice cream?" Jackson asked hopefully.

"Whipped cream." Her tone indicated take it or leave it.

"An old man can't even get ice cream with his cobbler anymore," he grumbled while Sara took away their dinner plates.

"I'm sure Elsie would be only too happy to serve you ice cream with your cobbler," she said sweetly, returning with three bowls of still-warm cobbler topped with whipped cream.

"I was just teasing," he said defensively, taking one of the bowls out of her hands and setting it in front of himself. The way he dug into his dessert with relish told them he really didn't mind that there wasn't any ice cream at all.

"You are a fine cook, Sara," Jess complimented after polishing off his second helping of dessert. "I can't understand why Tim and Jackson don't weigh three hundred pounds eating like this."

"Probably because she only cooks like this when we have company," Tim replied, standing up and clearing the table without Sara asking him to. She knew he was doing it to make a good impression and quite probably succeeding.

"I insist on helping with the dishes," Jess offered, rising from his chair and helping carry dishes into the kitchen. "I'm afraid if I sit down, I'll be asleep in minutes."

Tim brightened at the idea of getting out of his least favorite chore.

"That's very nice, Reverend, but after all you are company," Sara purred, sounding as sweet as cotton candy. Tim's face fell.

"Oh, but I insist," Jess told her, setting the dishes on the counter and rummaging beneath the sink for detergent.

"Since we have a dishwasher there's little to be done," she bit out, keeping her face frozen in a smile that was beginning to hurt from her efforts in keeping it in place.

"Then we'll finish all that much sooner, won't we? Ah, here it is!" He held the bottle of dishwashing liquid aloft. "First we'll load the dishwasher, then work on the pans. You wash, I'll dry."

Having him for a dishwashing partner was the last thing she needed, and as soon as Tim left the room she let him know it.

"I'm well aware of your game, and I don't like it," she muttered.

"I don't know what you mean." Jess was innocence personified.

"You know very well what I'm talking about, so don't act dumb with me. The way you covered my hand anytime I offered you something. The way you watched me eat dessert," she hissed, practically flinging the dishes in the dishwasher, little caring if any broke. "And you a minister, too. I wonder what some of your prim and proper members would have thought of your little antics today."

In one swift movement Jess turned the water off and spun Sara around, keeping his hands on her shoulders so she couldn't move away.

"I hadn't thought about our games in years," he admitted, "but sitting there across from you, I started to remember some of the good times we had, and maybe some part of me wanted to recall them again." His eyes bored into hers, wanting her to understand.

"We can't go back. We both know that." Sara felt an incredible sadness, because a part of her liked the idea of returning to that time of fewer worries in her life, but she was smart enough to know fate wouldn't allow that. But it didn't stop her from dreaming even for a moment.

"Mom!" They parted, each looking guilty as if they had been caught doing something wrong, but their eyes didn't leave each other's faces.

"Coming, Tim." Sara broke the eye contact first.

Tim was standing in the dining room with a worried look on his face.

"I can't believe you're doing it."

Her guilty half suspected the worst. "Doing what?"

"Making him do the dishes," he said in a low voice. "Mom, he's company, and you always said company doesn't do the dishes."

"I did not *make* him do anything," she told him. "He volunteered on his own, a gesture you could learn from."

"Yeah, but still, he shouldn't have to do the dishes."

Sara pushed him toward the kitchen. "Fine. You go in and tell him he's been relieved."

Caught neatly in his own trap, Tim sighed and gave in.

"I'll probably be the only kid in school with dishpan hands," he groused, then raised his voice when he entered the kitchen. "Come on, Preach, you can't have chapped hands. It'll ruin the image. I told Mom I'd finish them for you guys."

"Thanks, Tim." When Jess walked out of the kitchen, his expression was solemn, but his eyes danced with laughter. "Why do I have the feeling it wasn't his idea?" he whispered.

"Let's just say next time he'll think twice before speaking up."

Jess looked around. "Where's Jackson?"

"Snoring in front of the TV. He claims to one and all he loves baseball, but he always falls asleep before the end of the first inning," she said softly. "Why are we whispering?"

He grabbed her hand and pulled her toward the hallway. "We're whispering so no one knows we're sneaking out of the house for a walk," he confided.

"No, we're—" Her shriek of protest lowered. "No, we're not. You're here as Tim's guest, not mine."

Jess released her hand and walked back to the kitchen. "Tim, your mother and I are going for a walk to talk over your case."

"You can't do it here?" He sounded suspicious.

"Not when there's a smart-mouthed kid around with big ears," Jess said humorously. "By the way, that pan isn't too clean. You better do it again."

"Thanks again." Tim's sarcasm followed Jess as he regained Sara's hand and pulled her out of the house.

"We can't be seen together," Sara protested as he dragged her down a path.

"Like what? Are you throwing off your clothes and doing a pagan dance?" His lips quirked. "Are you trying to seduce me?"

"That's not funny!" Sara tried vainly to dig in her heels, but Jess wasn't going to allow her to pull back. "There are people in this town who would believe I was capable of such a thing and more."

Jess halted so suddenly Sara skidded to a stop and almost fell. "Take off the scarlet letter, Sara," he snapped. "That, along with the sackcloth and ashes, isn't becoming to you."

"The scarlet letter was for adultery," she pointed out.

He shook his head. "Who do you blame more in this, me or you? Sometimes I wonder if you're not happy playing the martyr."

She flushed. "You're wrong on that count," she protested in a low voice, her fists clenched at her sides, a clear sign of her agitation. "I don't allow anyone to make me feel guilty for having Tim, much less keeping him.''

"I never thought you did," he murmured, before moving off again. This time Sara followed on her own.

"You told Tim we were going to discuss his case," she prompted. "You don't want to be thought a liar, do you?"

He sighed. "No, I'm not going to lie about that." He looked around the grassy clearing situated a fair distance from the house and sat down Indian style, patting the spot beside him. "Pull up a chair."

She sat down curling her legs under her.

"About Tim," he went on. "One afternoon spent with him doesn't tell me all, but I have a strong idea he's very angry at the world and he's troubled."

"Thank you for telling me something I didn't know." Sarcasm laced her words. "Not to mention making my son sound like a novice psychopath. Next you'll tell me he's changing his name to Norman Bates."

"This is not a joke. He can't stand to upset or hurt you," he went on. "At the same time I don't think he truly knows how to stop. He's young, he has a hot temper, and he needs to learn how to control it."

"And you intend to show him." She clearly didn't believe him.

Jess nodded. "Sara, I went back to school and got a degree in psychology. I've worked with a lot of troubled kids over the years."

"Kids like Tim."

"Kids like Tim," he acknowledged. "I don't admit to having one hundred percent success, but I've dealt with enough kids to recognize the signs. I feel confident I can help Tim as long as the two of you let me work with him on a regular basis and he's willing to work hard.''

''Don't you mean if Judge Carmody allows you to work with him on a regular basis?'' She reminded him of the hearing that wasn't all that far off.

''If we play our cards right, I'll get that chance.''

Sara looked down at the pile of grass she had been methodically shredding during the past few minutes.

''What happened to you back then, Jess?'' Her whisper drifted with the breeze. ''Where did you go?''

''I went off to find myself,'' he said cryptically.

She sat up straighter. ''Why won't you tell me the truth? What secrets are you keeping from me?''

He looked up at her face, flushed pink from the heat and indignation. ''What secrets I have are mine to keep.''

Sara moved to get up, but Jess swiftly jackknifed upward, pulling her down beside him, threading his fingers through her hair so she couldn't escape.

''Why worry about the past when the present is more interesting?'' he murmured, pulling her face toward his. This kiss wasn't innocent or that of a young, eager lover. This was a man who once knew her intimately and drew upon those memories as he made a leisurely second meal of her mouth. Sara was beyond protesting. She was too busy melting against him, awash with the desire to rediscover his male contours. She forgot all but the man making her feel like a desirable woman again, and she only knew she wanted more as her body angled closer to his.

''As much as I like your idea, I don't think this is the place for it.''

As the meaning of his words sunk in, Sara could only feel mortification.

"I can't believe I..." She groaned, ducking her head.

"Showed you're a woman with feelings? Sara, we were once lovers, no matter what, we still share some of those old feelings," he explained, framing her hot cheeks with his hands and staring deep into her eyes.

"But you're our minister." She sounded appalled and disgusted with herself. "You're not the man I knew long ago."

No, he wasn't, he sadly admitted. That man had been literally reborn into someone who learned to care more for others than himself.

"So why can't two grown-up individuals meet, get interested in each other and perhaps even go on a date?"

Sara's distress with herself was promptly forgotten as she stared at him, unable to believe her ears. "No, Jess." She was determined not to say anymore.

He grabbed hold of her. "Give us a chance, Sara."

She drew back slightly. How tempting that would be, but at what cost? She wanted to refuse, but a part of her ignored her better judgment. Would it be so wrong?

"By my rules?" she asked, knowing she was setting herself up for a lot of pain if it all blew up in their faces.

"Rules?"

Sara nodded. "Surely you understand that no one can find out about us, at least not right away. This is a very delicate situation, and I don't want to see you hurt. I know what these people can say and do. If they found out Tim is your son, they'd grind you up and spit you out." She cupped his face with her hands, her fingertips tangled in his hair. In the bright sunlight she noticed the strands of silver among the dark and thought how distinguished they made him look.

"Sara, you have so little faith," he chided. "It's clear we were meant to be reunited so I could help you with Tim. What we have to do is take this one day at a time and see where it leads. Is that so difficult?"

She shook her head. Who couldn't have faith when he had so much to give?

"For your peace of mind we'll keep it very low-key." Jess lowered his voice. "You know what I mean. I come by your bedroom window at midnight and rap three times so you'll know it's safe."

Sara couldn't help it. She had to giggle. "This is the Jess I used to know," she pronounced, when she regained her self-control. She glanced down at his watch. "We should go back. I'm sure Tim is wondering where we've gone."

Jess agreed. He stood up and helped her to her feet. They held hands through most of their walk until they were in sight of the house. Then, by silent mutual agreement, they moved apart several feet.

"I'd like to talk to Tim for a few minutes before I go." Jess was the first to break their self-imposed silence.

"Of course." At that moment she would have granted him anything.

Jess tracked Tim down in his room, and Sara went into the den to wake up Jackson, who insisted he hadn't been asleep but merely resting his eyes. She remained with the older man until Jess appeared, delivering a polite thank-you for the meal and his promise to be present for Tim's hearing. Sara managed a bland smile and nod of her head for Tim's and Jackson's benefit. After Jess left she noticed her son didn't look as happy as he had earlier.

"Now you look as if you have a pile of homework, which you know I'll insist on your finishing," she teased.

"I just thought I'd have to go over there a couple times to prove to the judge I'm okay and that would be that," he blurted out. "It won't be that way at all."

"Ain't no free rides in life, boy," Jackson intoned. Sara rolled her eyes.

"That sure made me feel better," Tim jeered, before running out of the room.

"What's wrong, Sara? Don't you think the preacher can make everything right?" Jackson asked her. "The time had to come when Tim would learn he can't slide through life."

"I can't let him go to jail just so he can learn a lesson," Sara protested.

"No, that isn't the way, either, and I have an idea the preacher has a few good ideas up his sleeve, and they don't all concern Tim, either. But if he can get him straightened out, we'll all be happy." He then added, "Just as long as he don't make me go to church."

"No, I don't think he'll insist on that," Sara murmured. She knew Jess already had his part in the hearing figured out. She just wished she knew more about it. She remembered Jess's injunction that she have faith. He made it so easy, so why couldn't she feel as confident as he did?

Chapter Nine

Sara slept little the night before Tim's hearing. When she saw her pale skin and shadowed eyes in the bathroom mirror, she knew she would have to apply an extra layer of makeup in order to appear fresh and glowing, as so many cosmetic advertisements claimed. She hoped they were right, because she certainly didn't feel all that fresh and glowing. A wrung-out dishrag was more like it.

She dressed carefully in an off-white suit with an apricot blouse to add color to her still unnaturally pale cheeks. She entered the kitchen to find Tim eating cereal at the table.

"What is this?" she cried, staring at her son as if he'd suddenly sprouted a second head.

Tim looked up bewildered. "What is what?"

Her gaze flew over his uncombed hair, rumpled T-shirt and faded jeans. She was afraid to see what was on his feet.

"You can't be planning to see the judge dressed like that?" Sara wailed.

"You said I still had to go to school afterward, so I just put on what I wear to school."

She closed her eyes, slowly counted to ten and opened them. "You go back to your room, put on your brown slacks, a dress shirt and a matching tie. And comb your hair."

"I can't go to school wearing a tie," Tim protested.

"You'll wear a three-piece suit if I say so. I don't intend us to be late, so get going *now*!" Tim jumped, and Sara could have sworn she had never seen him move so fast as he bolted out of the room. "And brush your teeth," she called after him.

"I'm not six years old!"

"Anyone who dresses like that for a court hearing has the sense of a six-year-old." She poured a cup of coffee and lifted it with shaking hands.

"If you're not careful, you're gonna spill that all over your nice clothes," Jackson commented.

"I'm hoping it will calm my nerves," she said wryly, sipping the hot brew.

"I thought there was nothing to worry about."

"Tell that to my stomach." She looked up when Tim later ran in, now dressed to her specifications with his hair neatly combed. "I should have had you get a haircut," she mumbled, ushering him out to the car.

"Good luck," Jackson called after them.

"Can I drive?" Tim asked as they got into the car.

"No."

Tim knew this wasn't going to be easy when his mother rattled off instructions during the drive to the courthouse.

"Mom, I'll never be able to remember all you're telling me," he protested, slumping down in the seat.

"And sit up straight, don't forget to call him sir," Sara went on, but by then Tim had tuned her out.

He prayed the reverend didn't have further orders for him, because he was positive his brain was on overload.

"Give me a break, Mom," he groaned, climbing out of the car. "Either the judge lets me go, or he puts me in jail. It's one or the other, and there's nothing we can do to change it."

"That does not comfort me," she muttered. "Manners can go a long way to make a good impression." When something landed on her shoulder, she screamed and jumped away.

"Hey, it's only me," Jess said hastily for fear she'd lash out with her purse before she recognized him.

She stood there a moment, breathing heavily to restore her equilibrium. "You scared a good ten years off my life," she said slowly, pressing her hand against her rapidly thumping heart. "And I cannot afford even one."

"She's nervous," Tim confided in a man-to-man tone.

Jess nodded, noting Sara's pale features and rigid stance. If she was any stiffer, she'd break in half.

"Glad to see you dressed for the occasion, Tim," he told the boy.

"If you'd heard Mom this morning, you'd understand why it was safer not to wear jeans."

Sara studied the slip of paper she'd scribbled the information on.

"Room one-ten," she muttered, walking rapidly into the courthouse with her entourage on her heels.

"Don't let her talk to the judge," Tim pleaded to Jess under his breath. "She might start talking about when I was a baby or something."

"We'll see what happens," he replied absently, deciding he liked seeing Sara wear high heels. They did nice things for her legs. He found himself thinking about her more and more lately. He was well aware there could be complications for them, but he had endured other trials, and he knew they would emerge from this experience stronger. Now all he had to do was convince Sara of this.

Sara couldn't decide if they were better or worse off meeting in the judge's chambers. She settled on the latter when she met Judge Carmody.

He looked like a cross between John Carradine and Boris Karloff, she thought miserably, mustering up a faint smile as she shook hands with the dark-robed man with a face that had probably never cracked a smile in his lifetime. She shot Jess a look of desperation, but he merely smiled and winked at her. She did not feel all that assured as she glanced around the walnut-paneled office and couldn't find one item out of place or a speck of dust anywhere. Even his desk blotter didn't show any wear and tear, she thought sadly.

The judge fixed a steely-eyed glare on Tim, who shifted uncomfortably in his seat.

"Well, young man, you had yourself quite a time, didn't you?" Sara decided even his voice was from a B prison movie.

"Yes, sir, er, no, sir," Tim muttered, unsure exactly what to say.

"Yes or no, which is it? And speak up clearly," he barked.

"I, ah, I didn't mean to do it," Tim stammered, shifting uneasily in his chair.

Sara resisted the urge to bury her head in her hands. Hadn't he listened to one word she had said during the drive here? He could be so articulate if he wanted to be, and now...well, he wasn't making a very good impression.

"You didn't mean to severely damage a car and beat up several boys?" Judge Carmody said sarcastically. "Now why do I have trouble believing that?"

Sara stared at Jess, silently pleading for help.

"Judge Carmody, if I may say something?" Jess thought it was time he spoke up.

His head swiveled in Jess's direction. "And who are you?"

"I'm Pastor Jess Larkin. Timothy is a member of my church," he said smoothly, rising to his feet.

"So what do you have to do with this case?" he demanded. "Surely, you're not going to tell me how he's heavily involved in your church's youth group and he attends church every Sunday. From what I've read in this boy's file it's an open-and-shut case. He's incorrigible, the mother is single with no prospects for marriage, therefore no father figure around for him to learn from. I see no reason why he shouldn't be sent to a place where he'll learn how to behave properly."

Sara gripped the chair arms so tightly her knuckles were white. Dark spots appeared before her eyes, and she feared she was going to faint. It was much worse than she thought it would be. She would have spoken up, possibly saying something she would have regretted later, but Jess's firm hand on her shoulder stopped her.

"Let me explain further, Judge," he went on. "My previous work was in Atlanta working in a church-funded halfway house. I have a Ph.D. in psychology, and my specialization was counseling runaways and kids with severe emotional problems. Tim was wrong in reacting the way he did to the other boys' idea of a joke.

He's at a fragile age where he's neither a boy nor a man, and emotions can be a bit unstable. What I would like to propose is that Tim take an extra job to pay for the damages and that he undergo counseling to learn how to control his temper. This is his first offense, and we're both aware a structured facility isn't always beneficial for a boy."

The older man stared long and hard at Jess, gauging his sincerity. It was clear he trusted few people, and he was deciding whether or not Jess was one he could trust.

"And I suppose you're volunteering to counsel him?" He sounded skeptical.

"Yes, I am. Of course, if you'd care to check my credentials first, I would understand." He handed the judge several business cards. "These are the numbers of the head of the halfway house I worked in, several psychologists I shared a clinic with and two fathers of boys I counseled."

Judge Carmody barely glanced at the cards as he dropped them on his desk blotter. He leaned back in his chair, his fingers touching in a steeple shape at his lips as he stared long and hard at Tim, who bravely returned his stare.

"You'll be working pretty hard to pay the repair bills for that car, boy," he told Tim. "And I'll be checking the reverend's credentials thoroughly. And if they don't check out to my satisfaction, we'll be back here for another meeting you won't like one bit." He turned to Jess. "I'll expect a written report weekly. If the boy gets out of line once, if his grades aren't kept up, fun time is over, and he'll be sent to a correctional facility." He closed the file folder, indicating their time was up.

Sara stood up, her body trembling with repressed anger at both the judge and Jess. When she reached the door, she stopped and turned around.

"By the way, Judge Carmody, the 'boy's' name is Tim," she said quietly. "Perhaps if the boys you see were treated as individuals from the beginning, they would feel more like important citizens and less like a file number."

"Young woman, you are impertinent!" he blustered.

"No, I'm just a mother." With that she made a dignified exit.

"You took a chance in there," Jess informed her as the trio walked down the hall.

"He deserved it, and more," she said grimly. "But you deserve an award too. You made Tim sound like those juveniles you counseled and that his best hope was you." She halted and swung around to face him. "How dare you do that!"

"I dare anything that will keep him out of jail," he said, his hands planted on his hips, looking like the aggressive Jess she once knew. "You saw what the judge is like; he firmly believes even the first offenders should be locked up with the key thrown away. I did some checking up on him, so I knew what we would be up against, and I learned I was going to have to do some fast talking." He shook his head, exasperated with the pair standing before him. Couldn't Sara see what he was trying to do for them? For Tim?

"Sara, I was prepared to do anything I could for Tim in there," he whispered fiercely. "I had to. And you know exactly why. What did you expect, that Tim would get off with a slap on the wrist and his promise that he would never do it again? Stop and think about what almost happened in there and ask me again if I was too hard on Tim." His eyes challenged her, and there was something more than anger in their dark expression. There was also sorrow that she doubted him in the least when he had fought so hard for the boy he wanted so badly to call his son.

"I agree he should pay for the damages, but counseling?" Her eyes silently asked for his forgiveness.

"I'm not going to any kind of counseling," Tim broke in. "That's for nut cases."

Jess's gaze sliced his way. "Fine, then why don't I go back in there and tell Judge Carmody you refuse the conditions and to do with you what he will." He suddenly wished Tim was young enough for a good old-fashioned spanking, because that was clearly what the boy needed.

Tim panicked. "He'd send me away!"

Jess felt his temper slipping. "Then take your choice and make your decision quick. I will be giving up a lot of free time in hopes of knocking some sense into that thick head of yours, and if you and your mother don't like it, let's end the whole thing now." He glowered at them. "If it's all right with you, I don't intend to stick around here all day."

Tim eyed him suspiciously as he loosened the tie that was strangling him. "Why are you willing to do this for me? I mean you don't even know me."

Jess dropped his head, then slowly looked up. "Probably because I see a lot of me in you," he said quietly. "And I'd hate for anyone to go through what I did. As I said, if you don't like the deal, you can be the one to go in there and tell him. I have better things to do." Not even looking at Sara, he left them standing in the middle of the hall looking at each other.

"Well, what will it be?" Sara asked finally.

Tim thought about it. "Mr. Carson at the hardware store is looking for extra help, and I already have my work permit, so I'd probably have no problem getting the job."

Sara knew Jess was right, but a part of her still battled the idea that Tim needed professional help. Then she remembered Jess telling Tim he didn't want him to end up like him. Why didn't something add up?

"I'll drop you off at school on my way home," she said quietly.

For the rest of the day Sara mulled over Jess's words, but still couldn't come to a definite conclusion. Tim arrived home in the late afternoon with the announcement he had a job at the hardware store three afternoons a week and a half day on Saturday. He had also stopped by the minister's house and would be seeing him twice a week.

"What did he say?" Sara asked, trying to sound casual.

Tim shrugged. "Just that there would be times I'd hate him, but it would be understandable." His reply wasn't what she wanted to hear. "And he was going to show me alternate ways to work off my anger and frustration," he added, clearly unimpressed.

"Did he say any more about why he didn't want you to end up like him?" *Did he ask about me?*

He shook his head. "I go over there tomorrow. I'm hungry. When's dinner going to be ready?"

"In an hour. Will you go down and help Jackson until then?"

Sara waited until Tim left the house before calling Jess. Mrs. Harris's frosty voice informed her the reverend was in his study and wasn't to be disturbed, but

Sara refused to back down, and after a few moments Jess came on the line.

"Yes, Sara?" His tone was without any emotion. She could have been a perfect stranger.

"I wanted to apologize for this morning." She gripped the receiver tightly. "You're the expert in these matters, and I wasn't willing to listen to you after you had gone to all the trouble of going in there with us. I should have trusted you."

"Yes, you should have." He wasn't giving an inch.

"I thought ministers were supposed to preach about forgiveness." She tried to inject a light note.

"You're the one who swings from one end to the other," he reminded her. "First you're willing to see what chance we have, then you push me away. How am I supposed to take anything you say when I'm not sure what your next reaction will be?"

Sara winced. How she hated to admit he was right.

"After several sessions with Tim I'd like you to accompany him to a few," he informed her. "I'll let you know the days and times later. Thank you for calling." He carefully replaced the receiver in the cradle.

Jess hated to sound so cold to Sara, but he had to force her to see some sense. He freely admitted he had his own selfish motives in this; it gave him a chance to get to know his son and vice versa. At the same time he intended to get to know the new Sara and for her to get to know him also.

He looked around at the spare furnishings that made up his house. He then thought of Sara's home with its warm colors and homey atmosphere. Before, his house was considered a place to sleep, change his clothes and meet with members of his congregation. He had few personal mementos scattered around. Not like Sara's home, where side tables boasted photographs of Tim from newborn to present, a few of Sara and the walls were decorated with lithographs of waterfalls. The furniture was old and worn, but no one seemed to care. Their aura of the average family made him jealous, because he knew he could never be a part of it. Of course there was one way of barging into that family unit—give up his church and let everything out into the open. Talk about another continuing episode on that daily soap opera about the trials and tribulations of Henderson. But he knew he would never do it. His work came first, and while he was attracted to Sara all over again that would have to wait for awhile until he had a chance to work with Tim and see where it could all lead.

Jess closed his eyes, feeling an inner peace flow through him. Sara certainly wouldn't recognize this quieter side of him. He had grown to enjoy these times of meditation. He also thought fondly of Wayne, who had shown him the way. He missed his friend, who had died of cancer two years before. Jess would have wanted to call and talk to him about Sara. Perhaps Wayne would have had the answers Jess was looking for. He smiled. No, Wayne would just tell him to pray and search his own heart for the answers. It sounded so simple and was so complicated all in one fell swoop. Oh, well, it would fall into place soon enough. That was one thing he knew for sure.

TESS ARRIVED at the gas station bright and early the next morning bearing a plate of still-warm cinnamon rolls.

"Jackson, I'm stealing Sara for awhile," she announced. "I promised to sort through the new items for the missionary cupboard, and I knew Sara would be only too happy to help me." She smiled at Sara's stunned expression and rapid shaking of her head. "Wouldn't you?"

"I have a lot to do here," she argued.

"Nothing that needs the two of us." Jackson eyed the plate with a hungry gaze. "You two ain't going to eat all of them rolls by yourselves, are you? I'd sure hate to see you get fat."

Tess laughed as she set the plate on the workbench near him. "That's probably why I brought this along for a bribe."

Jackson wiped his hands on a rag and grabbed a roll, biting into its sweet stickiness. "Okay, you can take her."

"I can't believe I was given up so easily." Sara laughed as the two women walked over to Tess's car.

"What can I say? My cinnamon rolls have forced greater men to fall," Tess said airily, starting the car. "Now let's get this show on the road. I have a bone to pick with you, sweetie."

"I can't imagine I've committed a major crime. I just don't have the time for it," Sara admitted, fearing the worst.

Tess didn't say anything right away, but Sara knew better than to feel relieved. As soon as the two women arrived at the church and walked down to the basement where the children's Sunday School classes were held and over to a large cabinet that held various items given to visiting missionaries, Tess continued her complaints.

"You are supposed to be my best friend, the person who suffered right along with me through training bras, double-dating, the mother-daughter talks where we used to compare notes and a few other blackmailable items.

Now I have to learn from the grapevine that Tim beat up some kids, was arrested and thrown in jail, and our esteemed minister had Sunday dinner at your house. Do you know what it's like to get gossip secondhand? Especially when I have to act as if I already knew it all." Tess took out a stenographic notebook and began listing the new gifts. "Somebody actually gave five tubes of Muppets toothpaste?" she muttered, searching the contents of one of the large, brown paper shopping bags sitting by the cabinet. "Donations were certainly generous this time."

Sara chuckled as she lifted the toothpaste tubes. "They even threw in matching toothbrushes."

"So tell me what happened." Tess refused to be deterred for more than a moment.

"All right, I plead guilty. But the way things have been going lately, I'm lucky to get up in the morning."

"That is not telling me what happened."

Sara sighed. "A lot." As she handed her friend several boxes of men's after-shave and women's cologne, she related the story of Jess's dinner invitation and the evening spent in Charlotte and Tim's so-called invitation from Lora Summers. "Needless to say I was stunned when I came home to Jackson's announcement that Tim was in jail. The next day I took my hat in my hand and went to Jess, because I knew Tim would have to see Judge Carmody and he would need all the help he could get." She carefully folded a stack of dish towels and gave them to Tess, who carefully marked each item in a stenographic notebook.

"Oh, no," Tess groaned, then brightened. "But he isn't in jail now, or my grapevine isn't as efficient as it used to be."

"No, Jess will be counseling him," Sara explained, then giggled as she held up a lacy nightgown. "You have got to be kidding." The two women laughed softly as they guessed who might donate the sexy nightgown before Tess reverted back to Sara's slip of the tongue.

"Jess? My, my, we are chummy with the reverend, aren't we?"

"He only came over for dinner, and he's counseling Tim, nothing more," Sara said primly.

"That's all?" Tess jeered, holding the nightgown in front of Sara, who promptly snatched it away and folded it up, stuffing it in the back of the cabinet. She doubted it would be chosen.

"Tess, some things are private," she protested.

"My God, he kissed you," she guessed. "And, Sara, you kissed him back."

"Tess!"

"Sara Anne Murdock, you never could lie to me, so don't try now. Besides, your face is as red as a beet," she accused, then leaned forward. "Is he still a great kisser? I mean I figured he was a good kisser before, because you're all dreamy eyed, just from the memory no less, so he must have improved with age. And well, you can't have an affair with him, so you may as well kiss your brains out. Is that what you did?"

"Tess!" Sara was horrified by her friend's audacious statement, but she couldn't help laughing anyway.

"Well, you can't," she persisted. "It's almost the same as if he was a priest. Actually it's a good thing he isn't, or you'd really be out of luck."

Sara laughed so hard her sides hurt and tears ran down her cheeks. She grabbed the edge of the cabinet door for balance. "You're bordering on the sacrilegious there. Besides, Tess, you know very well nothing can happen between us.''

''Because of old lady Masterson and her coven?'' Tess showed her disdain. ''Look, Sara, you've done without for a lot of years. If you get the chance, take it and don't look back,'' she said earnestly. Checking the two grocery bags and seeing that they were empty, she folded them carefully and put them in the cabinet also.

''Jess and I talked, and we'll keep a low profile until we make a decision one way or another.''

''But that's not what you plan to stick to if you can help it.''

''Tess, I can't allow Jess to compromise himself. When the proper time comes, I'll tell Tim the truth about his father, but not while they're working together. I don't want Tim to lose his respect for Jess.'' They walked upstairs and out into the warm sunshine, where Tess dragged Sara over to her car and took out a covered plate and thermos.

They carried their snack over to a nearby tree and sat under the inviting shade. While they feasted on fresh cinnamon rolls and iced tea, Sara couldn't help but look around every so often as if she were afraid Jess would suddenly appear. Or hoped he would.

Tess contemplated the last roll before she picked it up, carefully tore it in half and offered one part to Sara.

''I read somewhere that people eat more when they're sexually frustrated,'' she said casually. ''Do you think that's true?''

Sara held Tess's piercing gaze as she slowly accepted the piece. ''Then I don't know why you bother eating at all. That's probably the least of your worries.'' She devoured the roll in two bites.

Tess chuckled. "The perfect solution to keep a husband from straying: make sure he's so tired he doesn't have the energy to look at other women."

"You have a very special marriage, Tess. Something to cherish," Sara told her seriously.

"Then go after your own special love."

"The time isn't right."

"Then make it right," she urged. "Sara, you can do anything you want. You know that."

She sipped her tea. "Can I? Sometimes I wonder. Jess and I lost each other once before. Who says it won't happen again?"

"Only if you refuse to look on the bright side."

"This has nothing to do with looking on the bright side, and you know it," Sara argued.

"Don't be a fool, Sara," Tess said in a sharper tone than she had ever used with her friend. "You've been given this second chance. Don't throw it away."

The two women stared at each other, neither refusing to give up.

"Please, Tess, I have to do this my way."

Tess opened her mouth, prepared to argue, but just as quickly closed it as if deciding now was not the time.

Chapter Ten

At first glance Sara knew Tim's first session with Jess had not gone well. He came home scowling and in a thoroughly rotten mood. She was prepared to overlook the mood until he began complaining about dinner.

"This is the fourth time we've had chicken in less than two weeks," he complained, picking at his meal. "Pretty soon I'm going to grow feathers and cluck."

"If you don't like it, you don't have to eat it," Sara pointed out tautly, putting her fork down. "All you've done since you've gotten home is complain about everything. You couldn't find clean jeans, a dry towel, and even your fork wasn't up to your new standards. I suggest you snap out of this quick or remain in your room for the rest of the evening."

He stared at her long and hard with Jess's eyes. Uttering an exasperated sound under his breath, he shoved his chair back and stalked out of the kitchen.

"He's sure got a tick up his—"

"Jackson!" Sara warned.

"I thought the preacher said these sessions were supposed to help him," he argued.

Sara sighed wearily. "I did, too."

"Then somebody better tell Tim that."

She knew very well who that person would have to be. She got up from the table and headed for Tim's bedroom. She knocked and waited for his invitation before entering.

"Tim, the day will come when I won't be able to find you among this mess," she commented, picking her way carefully over scattered clothing and books. She sat down on the bed beside him. "What was your session like?"

"Usual bull," he muttered, refusing to look at her.

"That makes a lot of sense. Do you talk about school, your friends, family, what?"

Tim bolted up. "Look, Mom, I don't want to talk about it, okay? We just talk about stuff."

Sara mentally backed off, realizing these sessions were going to have to be private, even from her.

Tim stared down at the book in his lap. "He likes me to talk about what I feel when I get angry," he said finally. "How the hell do I know how I feel when I'm mad? I don't think about anything then."

"Is that what you told him?"

"Yeah."

"What did he say?"

He grinned. "That he was glad I didn't give him some line about seeing bright colors or hearing voices. I guess some kids do that."

"Tim, these sessions are very important for you. Do you understand?" she asked, touching his shoulder.

"Yeah, but it doesn't mean that I have to like them."

Sara agreed. "Have you started your homework?"

"Not yet."

"I'll leave your plate in the oven in case you change your mind." Sara rose to her feet and left the room. She couldn't remember ever feeling as helpless as she did now. How much of this could be her fault?

Her evening turned out uneventful after washing the dishes and throwing a load of laundry into the washer.

"I think I'm goin' out to California and get on *Wheel of Fortune*," Jackson announced from the den.

"That should be entertaining," she said under her breath.

"Yeah, and maybe Vanna White would kiss me." He chuckled at the idea.

"Jackson, you've always said you'd never fly," she reminded him. "How do you expect to get out there, because I doubt your truck would make it?"

"That's what trains are for," he persisted. "I'm an old man and should have one good thing happen to me 'fore I die."

"I wouldn't worry about my mortality if I were you," she said drily. "Only the good die young, so you're guaranteed a very long life."

"You're still a smart mouth, missy." He flipped the television remote control to another channel. "There's a Duke Wayne movie on," he announced with great relish, settling back in his chair.

Knowing how he liked the company, Sara curled up on the couch and watched the film with him.

It wasn't until she was getting ready for bed that she thought of Jess again. Acting on impulse, she dialed his number.

"Pastor Larkin here."

She said tentatively, "Jess, it's Sara. I didn't disturb you, did I?"

"No, Sara. I was just catching up on some reading. What can I do for you?"

She settled back in bed, cradling the receiver against her shoulder.

"I guess it's too early to ask how Tim is doing." She plumped her pillows behind her.

"Yes, it is." Silence. "Sara, why did you really call me?"

She decided this was no time to by coy. "I wanted to talk to you."

"About what?"

"You, me, us, the state of world affairs, the price of peaches."

He laughed as she hoped he would. "Okay, why don't you tell me how your day went?"

"You couldn't find a more interesting subject?" she quipped. "All right, here goes. I helped Jackson install a new carburetor, changed the oil in a car, cooked the requisite number of meals, washed a couple loads of laundry. Just a regular day in the Murdock household."

"Sounds busy to me," Jess commented, relaxing in his chair, fully prepared for a long talk if she was. "Is the laundry what you do for fun?"

"No, my fun time was watching a John Wayne movie with Jackson." Sara started to laugh softly. "You know, I feel as if I'm back in high school making those late-night calls after my parents thought I was in bed."

"Except now you're the parent making sure the kids are in bed, although in your case it's only one," he replied. "How was Tim's attitude when he got home?"

"Basically nothing I do is right, and he's mad at the world."

"Mad at me."

"That, too, I'm sure."

For a moment there were only sounds of their breathing over the telephone wires as each debated what to say next.

"I guess I should let you go," Sara said finally, unable to think of anything further to say without sounding ridiculous. "It is late."

"Sara, I'm glad you called," he said. "I hope you'll feel free enough to call me again or won't mind if I call you sometimes."

Her smile was echoed in her voice. "I'd like that."

"Sleep well."

"You, too." Her whisper just barely reached his ears.

They both hung up feeling as if a first step had been taken.

"THE DISHES BELONG in the sink, not on the table," Sara reminded her son as she hastily cleaned the kitchen before she left for the gas station. She grimaced when he casually tipped them into the dishwater and sauntered out the door with a goodbye wave. She would have said more, but the phone rang, and Tim was already gone.

"Hello?"

"Sara?"

Her heart skipped a beat.

"I heard there's a stand of trees on the east end of the lake that's pretty private. Meet me there at one o'clock," Jess told her.

"I can't leave Jackson alone," she protested, knowing she could and would.

"Yes, you can. Consider it our first counseling session. I'll see you then." He hung up before she could protest further.

Sara stood there staring at the receiver, the hum of the dial tone now reaching her ears. She carefully replaced the receiver in the cradle and left the house. She knew no matter what, she'd be at the lake at one o'clock.

At twelve-thirty Sara went up to the house to fix Jackson a sandwich and to pack a separate lunch for herself with an extra special surprise for Jess.

"I'll be back later this afternoon," she said, taking his meal down to him.

He eyed her sharply. "You're gonna see him, aren't you?"

Sara nodded, knowing there was no use in lying to him.

Jackson rubbed his hand over his chin. "I don't want to see you hurting anymore."

She smiled and kissed his cheek. "I don't worry about it as long as I've got you around." She ran over to her car carrying a wicker basket.

"Yeah, but I won't be around forever," he yelled, then swore at the familiar bell-like sound that warned him a car had driven alongside the gas pumps. "All right, all right, hold your pants on. Man can't even eat his lunch in peace anymore."

When Sara arrived at the lake, she was relieved to find only Jess's Bronco parked there. She knew the area was virtually deserted during the week, especially this end of the lake, since fishing wasn't accessible. She grabbed the basket and climbed out of the car. Jess, who had been sitting on one of the large rocks at the water's edge, looked up. He slid down and walked over to her.

"We're crazy." Sara said one thing, but her eyes held an entirely different message.

"So we've regressed sixteen years," he tossed back, standing in front of her and just allowing his eyes to take their fill of her sunshine beauty.

She held the basket up like a prize. "Nothing fancy: chicken-salad sandwiches, chocolate cake, some fruit and lemonade."

He threw back his head and laughed. A few strides took him over to his truck, where he pulled out a similar style basket and a heavy blanket, which he laid out on a bare spot of ground.

"Mrs. Harris's oatmeal cookies, ham and cheese sandwiches, iced tea and cut-up vegetables."

"It sounds like we're going to have a feast here." She set the basket down in the middle of the blanket and kneeled beside it. Jess sat down across from her with his basket as they retrieved their booty and proceeded to share.

"No one can make oatmeal cookies like Mrs. Harris," Sara decided, munching on her second cookie. "One of her secrets is a touch of cinnamon, but I've never been able to figure out the other. Do you realize a majority of the women in this town have a speciality? Mrs. Harris has her oatmeal cookies, Tess, her cinnamon rolls. Mrs. Lawrence makes fantastic potato salad, and Mrs. Baker fixes a pot roast that melts in your mouth."

"And what are you known for?"

She tipped her head to one side in thought. "I guess for me it's a toss-up between my chocolate-chip cheesecake and pasta salad."

He sadly studied her offerings. "And you didn't bring either."

Sara smiled as she handed Jess a chicken-salad sandwich and received a ham and cheese in return. "I didn't want to spoil you right off the bat."

"What did you do this morning?" She chose a carrot stick to accompany her sandwich and a plastic cup of lemonade. They had laughed when both realized they had forgotten napkins.

"I drove over to the retirement home and held a bible study." Jess began his second sandwich.

"Did you have a large turnout?"

He nodded. "Yes, twenty to twenty-five people, most of them in wheelchairs, but very enthusiastic. I enjoy my time with them." He chuckled, remembering something. "In fact, a couple of the ladies have volunteered to find me a wife. They feel everyone should be married. Maybe I should give them your name," he teased.

Sara wrinkled her nose. "I doubt they'll be able to find someone in Henderson." She grabbed the remaining piece of chocolate cake before Jess could nab it. "Oh, I almost forgot. I brought you a surprise." She rummaged in the bottom of the picnic basket and pulled out a large leather-bound book. "Voilà!" She handed him the book with a theatrical flourish.

Jess looked down at the book in his hands and then at Sara.

"Open it," she urged, smiling broadly. "I promise nothing will pop out at you."

Jess opened to the first page and murmured a prayer under his breath as he gazed at a Polaroid photograph of a wrinkled and red-faced newborn baby. This was not the beautiful pink-cheeked, smiling baby of magazine ads, but he doubted he had ever seen a more stirring sight. Neatly printed underneath was Tim's name, the date, his weight and time of birth. He swallowed a large lump in his throat, but it refused to budge. It was so difficult to equate this tiny blanket-shrouded bundle with the gawky boy he had come to know. He hadn't expected it to hurt so much that he hadn't been there to greet his son when he entered the world. For the first time in his life he felt like crying.

"He was a big baby," was all he could think to say in a raspy voice as he thought how slender Sara was. How had she managed to give birth? It was a stupid question to ask himself, he knew, but the thought of her suffering a lot of pain hurt him, too. He dropped the album into his lap when he realized his hands were trembling. He couldn't lift his head, because he didn't want Sara to see the pain in his eyes.

"And he let the entire world know he had arrived. The doctor said there was certainly nothing wrong with his lungs," she mused, remembering the first time she had held her child and counted his fingers and toes as only a new mother does.

Jess slowly turned the page to find pictures of a younger-looking Sara holding Tim. With each page he was treated to a continuing record of Tim's life helped by Sara's monologue. He breathed deeply through his nose, but it didn't help the emotions racing through his body and the tears burning his eyes.

"Once he learned how to walk, he couldn't be held back," Sara told him, now sitting close beside him. "Jackson used to say Tim ran on more cylinders than a race car."

Jess traced the edge of one photograph where a gap-toothed Tim presided over a birthday cake. Had it been a happy day for the boy? Did he have fun? He wished he had been there.

"A part of me feels sorrow at missing these important times in his life," he murmured. "And another part screams out, because I feel as if I'm looking at a perfect stranger."

"In a way you are," she said gently, understanding his dilemma. "After all, you didn't know about Tim then. Please don't feel bad, Jess. I brought the album so you could see what he was like as a baby. I thought you might enjoy it. I didn't intend to cause any guilt trips."

"I do enjoy it, although I can't imagine this holds fifteen years of his life."

"No, this only goes up to his seventh birthday."

With each new page Sara always had a tale to relate, such as Tim's first experience with a neighbor's puppy.

"He couldn't understand why he had to wear a diaper, and the puppy didn't when they were both considered unhousebroken," she laughed.

Jess chuckled. "Smart kid."

"Yes, but you weren't there when he tried to put a diaper on the cat we had then after the puppy had gone home. He decided the cat could wear one as long as he had to," she said drily. "She laid her claws into him, and he screamed like the holy terror he was. He's hated cats ever since."

"When I was eight, I dressed my dog in a pillowcase doubling as a cape," Jess reminisced. "I wanted to see if he could fly like Underdog."

Sara's eyes grew huge. "Fly? Such as pushing him off a roof or something?" she squeaked.

He nodded. "The idea sounded great to me. My mother caught me before I could inflict any damage, and I couldn't sit down for a week."

"That is terrible!"

"Boys do crazy things, what can I say?" Jess studied the last picture of Tim in the album. The boy was dressed in a navy blue suit and tie, his hair slicked back. The only jarring note was his very apparent black eye. He traced it with his fingertip, then closed the book. He turned to Sara, cupping her chin with his fingertips. "Thank you," he said huskily.

Sara only smiled, not feeling the need for words just then.

He thought of the inner strength it must have taken for her to raise her child alone. He cradled her face between his palms, his thumbs brushing her cheekbones with the lightest of touches as his head slowly lowered and tipped to one side. But his mouth didn't touch hers at first. Instead it applied butterfly kisses across each eyebrow, the closed eyelids, then down her nose before resting against her parted lips.

"You're taking too long," Sara murmured, linking her arms around his neck and pulling him down. This time she took charge, nibbling along his lower lip until her tongue gained entrance. She murmured softly as she searched out the dark moist cavern of his mouth. Jess moaned as his arms went fully around her, pulling her tightly against him, and he buried his face against her hair.

"So good," he muttered, when they came up for air.

"You always were." She couldn't resist teasing him.

Jess's mouth returned to hers, harder than ever. His hands roamed across her back and down to the curve of her backside before sliding back up to settle under the curves of her breasts, but not touching them.

"You're fuller than before," he murmured, afraid to touch her further. He felt as if his body was pulling him in two different directions as he remembered times past and his conscience reminded him of his teachings. He couldn't believe the attraction could escalate so strongly.

"Motherhood does that." She looked up at him with her feelings apparent on her face. She could tell he felt the same way.

Inhaling sharply, Jess released her and spun around. He raked his fingers through his hair and breathed deeply to calm his raging nerves. "We should probably get back," he muttered.

Nodding, Sara picked up the trash and packed it away in its respective hampers.

"Perhaps we should confine our conversations to the phone from now on," she said softly, feeling the shock waves as much as he did.

Jess shook his head. "While I enjoy talking to you on the phone, I also like to look at your face. Perhaps we could turn this into a regular date."

"All right." Sara carried her basket to her car and set it in the trunk, prepared to leave without anything more said.

"Sara." She turned around. "Could you bring the second album with you the next time?"

"I won't forget it," she promised. "Except next time you have to talk about yourself, too."

He held out his hand. "It's a deal." Looking very solemn, they shook hands before getting into their cars to go their separate ways.

While Mrs. Harris thought it strange that Pastor Larkin wasn't hungry for dinner and spent a lot of time sitting in his study looking off into space, Jackson wasn't a bit surprised by Sara's lack of appetite. If anything, he expected it, and he worried even more about her.

WHEN TIM ARRIVED at Jess's house for his second session, he was sullen and uncooperative from the beginning. Jess recognized the signs right away and took him outside.

"I don't see where this will do any good," Tim said, while Jess rummaged in the dark confines of the garage.

"They won't unless you want them to. Ah, here it is." He walked outside carrying a basketball.

Tim rolled his eyes. "That sounds like a line out of a movie."

"I guess it is. Who cares, as long as it gets my point across," Jess said quietly. "I went to your school yesterday and talked to some of your teachers." He closed the garage door and tossed the ball upward toward the basket. It bounced twice around the rim and gently slid down without going inside.

"That must have been fun."

He ignored the sarcasm as he threw the ball to Tim. "You're not some dumb kid, Tim. Your test scores are high, while your grades are barely passing. You go to class, but you don't listen. You have few friends, and they're all screwups like you want to be. You don't participate in school activities. And your first interest in the opposite sex turned out to be a disaster."

Tim reddened at that statement, then turned on him. "You think you're so smart, don't you? You talk to all those teachers who really don't give a damn about me, and now you think you know everything, but you don't." He ran backward several paces and threw the ball with little effort, the sphere dropping neatly into the basket.

"That was pure luck," Jess muttered, then added, "Then why don't you tell me what I don't know."

Tim sent the ball his way, throwing it just a bit too hard. If Jess hadn't caught it, it would have hit him squarely in his midsection. Jess looked at him for a moment, but said nothing. "Like I said, you think you know it all. Mom was never married to my dad, and a lot of creeps in this town like to remind me of it."

"And it bothers you." He jumped up, making a dunk shot and grinned smugly.

"Not me!" he denied hotly. "It's the things they say about Mom I don't like."

"Do they always say something about your mother?" he asked quietly, rolling the ball from one hand to the other.

Tim thought about it as he studied the frayed hem of his jeans. "No," he admitted finally. His head snapped up, his eyes blazing with anger. "But that's what they mean!"

"How do you know that?"

"Because they do!" he insisted, but he didn't sound as convincing this time.

Jess remained quiet, allowing Tim to mull over what he'd just said. He threw the ball back to Tim, who stood back even farther and made another basket.

"I wanted to think they said something about Mom," Tim whispered, shaking his head to deny what his mind had already figured out. "That really makes me a jerk."

"No, just the man of the family protecting his womenfolk," Jess said. "It's a male instinct, but one you have to learn to temper at times."

By then Tim had regained his old cockiness. "I thought you were going to teach me how to work that out," he challenged. "Or is that what you're doing now? Playing basketball doesn't do anything."

"Except to show me you're a much better player," he admitted wryly. "I will show you, as soon as I feel you're ready."

"Ready for what?"

"Ready to learn." Jess eyed him as he bounced the ball on the driveway several times before throwing it toward the basket. He grimaced when he missed. "Who knows? That time could be coming very soon."

Tim's curiosity was now aroused, but Jess wasn't about to indulge him just yet. For the next half hour they concentrated on just throwing baskets and finding out a bit more about each other.

SARA WAS RELIEVED TIM'S MOOD was better after this session. She was especially surprised when he offered to help her with the dishes. Afterward he mumbled he had homework and went to his bedroom.

"You better take that boy's temperature 'cause he's got to be sick," Jackson announced when Sara walked into the den.

"Maybe he's beginning to learn," she replied, curling up on the couch and picking up a book she had been meaning to read. "Why aren't you on your way to your poker game? Usually you're the first one there."

His eyes narrowed. "Why? You going to have company here or something?"

"Just my regular weekly orgy," she said airily, opening her book. "And you know how they hate to start late."

"This town should be so lucky," Jackson muttered, slowly rising from his chair. "Don't have too wild a night," he advised sarcastically. "It's your turn to open the station in the morning."

"Don't fleece the guys too much," she called after him.

After the house was quiet again, she mentally tossed a coin to decide whether to call Jess or just to wait and hope he'd call her, but before the imaginary coin finished its spin in the air, the phone rang.

"What a sweet man, now I don't have to appear too aggressive by calling him." She ran for the phone only to have it be one of Tim's friends. "Tim, telephone and make it short!"

"Can I take it in your bedroom?"

"Yes, as long as you keep it short, as in no more than ten minutes." So much for hoping it was Jess. She returned to her book.

It wasn't until two hours later when Sara finally emerged from her reading that she discovered Tim still on the phone and ordered him off by calmly placing her finger on the button and disconnecting the caller.

"This is a great deal longer than ten minutes," she informed him. "I dread to ask how much homework you have left to do."

He smirked. "It's all done."

"This is a first," Sara mumbled.

"Mom, I'm fifteen, not a kid anymore," Tim pointed out.

She peered closely at his face. "I can't handle this," she practically wailed. "I see at least three hairs on your chin. Before we know it you'll be shaving every morning."

His eyes lit up, and he dashed into her bathroom. "Hey, this is great!" He appeared in the doorway. "Say, Mom, is it okay if I buy a razor tomorrow?"

Sara visualized three additional gray hairs on her head to equal the three hairs on Tim's chin. She was right; she wasn't ready to handle this at all.

Chapter Eleven

Sara groaned when she looked outside to watch her first customer of the day pull up alongside the pumps. She knew the pale blue nineteen fifty-two Chevrolet as well as she did the owner. She was aware the car's engine was kept in mint condition thanks to a mechanic in Charlotte—heaven forbid that the car had to enter this gas station for anything other than sustenance—and its body kept shiny with a weekly wash and wax. She saw the gray-haired driver sitting behind the wheel, looking as majestic as Queen Victoria and with a will of iron that would equal the hull of a battleship. Sara stood up and walked out of the office.

"Good morning, Mrs. Masterson." She smiled at the somberly dressed woman, who barely looked at her.

"Fill it up, please." For all these years Sara couldn't remember the older woman ever calling her by name.

She nodded and unscrewed the gas cap. While the gas pumped away, Sara washed the windows and asked if she would like the oil checked.

"No, thank you, my mechanic takes care of that."

"Of course," Sara murmured, moving away when the gas pump clicked off. "That will be $16.72." She accepted the twenty dollar bill and hurriedly made change.

"I understand Pastor Larkin is trying to rehabilitate your son," Mrs. Masterson commented.

Sara held back her surprise that she had actually initiated a conversation. "He's counseling him, yes. I'm grateful to him for that."

The older woman looked at her with eyes cold as ice. "Just don't be too grateful. One mistake is about all this town could take."

She felt as if her face had been slapped and wasn't about to stand for it. "Mrs. Masterson, for years you have put myself and my son down for something that is really none of your business," she said tautly. "And, surprisingly, I've taken it, but no more. It's probably narrow-minded people like you who have caused Tim to feel so much anger. Now I don't expect to be invited to your Thursday-afternoon teas or the Wednesday-morning Ladies' Club, but I would like to be treated like a human being and not something the cat dragged in. If that can't be accomplished, then I suggest you find another source for your gas. Such as your precious mechanic!" With that she stalked away, head held high and back straight.

"Just don't drag that nice man down to your level, young woman," Mrs. Masterson called after her. "He has no idea what kind of person you really are."

Sara was tempted to tell the woman a few choice tidbits about the nice pastor. She spun around. "Neither do you," she stated quietly, standing her ground. "You never cared to find out, did you?"

Mrs. Masterson stared at her for several moments before turning back to turn on the engine, which purred to immediate life.

Sara remained in her spot, watching the aged car slowly drive away. She felt the tension creeping up her spine and knew she would probably have a headache for the rest of the day because of a confrontation she didn't need. At the same time she felt freer than she had in years. For the longest time she had always been just a bit in awe of the town's social leader and never would have dared to stand up to her. Yet she had, and she was still in one piece! Laughing, she threw her fist up in the air in triumph.

"If you want the town to think you've gone off your rocker, you're doin' it the right way," Jackson said from behind.

"Why not?" she giggled, spinning around. "Jackson, I did it!"

"Did what?" He looked at her suspiciously. "Have you been in the whiskey?"

"No, but I did tell Mrs. Masterson off," she stated with a broad grin.

Now Jackson stared at her even harder. "You told Cora where to go?"

She grimaced at him. "I didn't go that far. But I did tell her to mind her own business where Tim and I were concerned."

Jackson chuckled. "Glory be, you finally got some backbone where that woman's concerned. Just remember that she has a memory like an elephant and can strike back like a snake when least expected."

"Then let her. I'm tired of all her veiled threats and innuendos," she complained. "And when she brought Jess into it, I decided I'd had enough."

"The truth is gonna come out sooner or later, Sara," he warned. "And you'll have to be strong enough to stand up to even more malice than you knew when you were pregnant.''

It seemed her happiness was destined to be short-lived. "It would ruin Jess's career," she whispered.

"Then I say you ought to talk this out with him."

She nodded. Her first inclination was to call him, but fear that Mrs. Harris might be the one to pick up the phone stopped her. No, she had to be more careful now. Jackson was right, she would have to handle herself more carefully when around Jess.

Luckily she didn't have to wait too long. Jess pulled into the gas station later that morning.

"You can wait on this customer, darlin'," Jackson drawled with a broad grin.

Pasting a calm expression on her face, Sara walked out to the pumps. "Good morning, Reverend," she greeted him, watching him start the pump. "My, you're well trained. This station has remained pretty much full serve during these liberated times."

Jess leaned against the rear fender of his truck, his arms crossed in front of his chest, too busy enjoying the view before him to reply. Sara in faded jeans and a formfitting, pale green T-shirt was a feast to his eyes. Suddenly another picture flashed before his eyes. Sara, with short curlier hair, wearing nothing more than a smile. A smile directed at him. And just as quickly the picture was gone. He straightened up, searching his mind for something, anything to say.

"You'll be at the Marcys' anniversary party Friday night, won't you?"

Her eyes looked shadowed with something he would have sworn was pain. "No, I won't be."

"You weren't invited, were you?" he guessed correctly.

"They're very close friends of Mrs. Masterson." She managed a smile. "I'm used to it, Jess. And actually only a small faction of the town feels this way. If there had been more people who felt about me so strongly, I definitely would not have stayed."

"Then I'd like you to go to the party with me."

Sara's eyes widened with shock. "No, Jess. If you want to take someone with you, choose anyone but me."

He shook his head as he pulled the nozzle out of the gas tank. "I've chosen who I want to take, and it's you."

"You're still new here, you don't understand...."

"I'll pick you up at seven." He glanced at the pump and pulled his wallet out of his back pocket.

"I'm not going," she protested, but he was beyond hearing.

"The time has come for you to face them all, Sara." He handed her the money and walked around to the driver's door.

"Time for what? Jess!" She took several steps forward, but he had already started the engine and driven off. "Damn you!" she cried.

"Bad luck to cuss out a preacher," Jackson called out from the garage.

"He's crazy."

"Crazy about you, I'd say."

"He wants me to go with him to the Marcys' party." She turned to the older man for the empathy she knew she would receive.

"Maybe it's time."

Sara was about ready to grind her teeth. "What is all this talk about it being time?" she demanded. "First

Jess, and now you. Don't you realize what will happen if he shows up there with me?''

"I don't expect the roof will fall in if you show up." He chuckled. "'Course Cora might have a conniption fit. I'd sure like to see that."

"Maybe Jess could tell them that he's trying to re-form me, and he thought getting me out among 'good' people would help." She tried a weak attempt at humor.

"Like Sadie Thompson."

"That's a very old story. Besides, she seduced the preacher."

She could see a wicked twinkle in his eye and silently swore she should have seen it coming. "This time around let him seduce you. He did it once, he can do it again."

"I don't think Dear Abby will have any competition from you," she said drily.

"Huh, what does she know?" he snorted. "I've written that woman a lot of letters over the years giving her good advice, and I haven't seen one printed."

"Probably a good reason why she never did," Sara murmured under her breath.

"I heard that!"

"I know," she sang out.

Sara spent the afternoon catching up on her housework and doing her grocery shopping, not one of her favorite chores. As she walked through the store, she met several women she knew and liked and just as many she wasn't overly fond of.

"Martha, are you going to the Marcys' party?" one woman called over to a friend, pointedly ignoring Sara, who was standing nearby.

"Of course. I wouldn't miss it." She also snubbed Sara. "What are you going to wear?" From there the conversation turned to the pink silk versus the yellow jumpsuit.

By the time Sara left the store, she was ready to spit nails.

"Fine. If that's the way they want to be, I can fight back just as hard," she muttered, practically tossing the bags into the trunk of her car.

Sara was still in a bad mood when Tim arrived home from his job at the hardware store. Guessing it wouldn't be a good idea to tease her out of it after she snapped at him for closing the door too hard when he came in, he retreated to his room to do his homework. Even during dinner she answered in monosyllables and glared at Jackson who cackled every now and then.

"What's wrong with her?" Tim whispered to Jackson when Sara left them to do the dishes.

"She's learning about life, my boy."

Now feeling even more confused, Tim retreated to the den and listened to pots and pans rattle in the kitchen and an occasional muttered curse.

Sara would have preferred to ignore Friday night's event, but she wasn't allowed to. Tess called her every morning to remind her to wear her aqua dress, and each time Sara politely hung up on her. Jess called once to talk about Tim and remind her what time he'd pick her up. As for Jackson, he just made the suggestion that she might want to make appointments to have her hair done, get a manicure and whatever else a woman might do before a party. She ignored him.

"What is all this about some party you're going to?" Tim asked her Friday afternoon when he came home after his appointment with Jess and found Sara in her bedroom hanging her dress up on the door.

She drew a deep breath. "Reverend Larkin asked me to attend a party with him," she said quietly.

He looked as if he didn't quite believe her. "The preacher asked you out on a date?"

"It's not a date per se. He just asked me to attend a party with him," Sara repeated, not sounding like she was looking forward to it.

"Where?"

She hesitated. "The Marcys'."

Tim laughed harshly. He was well aware of the so-called social barriers. "The Marcys'? Come on, Mom, we both know they don't think too much of us. Why would you want to go there?"

"Yes, well, maybe Reverend Larkin feels that it's time for me to confront them so they understand I'm every bit as good as they are," she said, feeling uncomfortable under his scrutiny.

"Does he think it's going to do any good?" His tone implied he didn't think so.

"I guess it wouldn't hurt," she explained, knowing she was committed to attend the party.

"I hope not. But, Mom, dating the preacher?" Tim shook his head, clearly not thinking that was such a good idea, either.

"It is not a date," Sara protested, wishing she could get him off the subject.

Tim stared at her. "When a guy asks you to attend a party with him and he comes to pick you up, it's a date."

"All right, Tim, it's a date. I'm not going to argue with you tonight." Sara pulled her robe out of the closet. "Now if you don't mind, I want to take a bath and get ready."

"You always said you like showers better."

She tipped her head back, her eyes closed. "Tim, you are trying to pick a fight with me for some reason, and I'm not going to allow you to," she said in a low voice. "Jackson said he would take you out for dinner and a movie."

"To keep me out of the way?"

"Whatever way you want to look at it." Sara literally pushed him out of her room and closed the door after him.

After taking a moment to compose herself, she ran her bathwater and sprinkled scented oil in it. After twisting her hair on top of her head, she forced herself to relax in the warm, bubbly water. Her stomach was churning, but she refused to give in to an attack of nerves at this late date. The aqua dress, along with the white, beaded choker she chose to wear, accented her eyes. The more she looked in the mirror, the more convinced she became the reflection couldn't be the Sara Murdock she saw every morning when she washed her face.

Her eyes looked bluer, her skin glowed, her rose-glossed lips parted with expectation, and the soft waves of her hair lovingly framed her face. She transferred her personal items into a small, white, leather purse that matched the strappy high-heeled sandals she wore.

When she walked into the den, Jackson looked up and wolf whistled at her.

"That's the way you *should* look," he told her, then looked at Tim. "Right?"

The boy barely glanced up at her. "Yeah."

Sara walked over to him, using her thumb and forefinger to lift his chin. "I'm the same person, Tim," she said quietly. "I'm beginning to think that everyone is right, it *is* time for me to get out and face the rest of my personal demons. I think Reverend Larkin understands some of my problem, and he wants to help me overcome it."

"That's probably not all he wants to help you with," he muttered.

Sara's body jerked with shock at his crude remark. For a moment she was sorely tempted to tell him exactly how much she didn't appreciate it, but knew that would only alienate him further.

"I hope you'll be polite to the pastor when he arrives," she said instead.

"Why? Will he put me in jail if I don't?" He jumped out of his chair and ran out.

"We're leaving in five minutes," Jackson called after him, then lowered his voice. "He's hurting, Sara."

"He was fine until he heard who I was going out with," she sighed.

"I'll talk to him," he told her. "You haven't gone out with a man for a long time now, and I think he feels threatened."

"Who have you been listening to, Donahue or Winfrey?" she asked whimsically.

He scowled. "You want to learn something worthwhile, you listen to Dr. Ruth." He raised his voice to shout, "Come on, Tim! Otherwise we won't have enough time to eat before the first show."

Sara felt relieved that Tim didn't make any more nasty remarks before he left, except to question whether she'd be home early. She knew Jackson was right, her son was hurting, and maybe deep down he sensed this man was entirely different from the others she had seen in the past. How could she reassure him not to worry when she wasn't sure what was going to happen herself?

For the next fifteen minutes Sara wandered around the house, afraid to sit down and unsure what to do with herself. Why had she gotten ready so early when she should have known that she wouldn't have anything to do until Jess arrived? She almost sobbed with relief when the doorbell rang. Still she took several deep breaths and walked slowly to the door, opening it.

"Hi." She suddenly felt very shy. Jess wore navy slacks and jacket and a silver-gray dress shirt with the collar left open. "Would you like to come in?" She stepped back.

Jess was too busy looking over this new Sara and liking very much what he saw before him.

"You look lovely," he said huskily, his dark eyes roaming over her bare shoulders and down her slender figure. Standing so close to her he could smell the light fragrance of her cologne. "You should wear your hair down more often."

She touched the soft curls self-consciously. "This style isn't safe to wear around the garage."

"I'm surprised you didn't leave it short."

Sara shrugged. "It got to be too much of a pain to go in for a haircut every six weeks, so I just let it grow out."

Or she couldn't afford it, Jess thought. He reached out and touched a curl that curved near her cheek. "I think we better go," he suggested.

She nodded. "I'll get my purse."

Sara's high heels wouldn't allow her a graceful entrance into Jess's Bronco, so she finally laughed and slipped her shoes off, tossing them into the truck before she allowed him to assist her inside.

"I rarely get to wear pretty shoes anymore, and I forget they do have their drawbacks," she said, hooking her seat belt as Jess slid behind the wheel and switched on the engine.

"Women with gorgeous legs should wear pretty shoes," he quipped.

Sara half turned in the seat so she could face him. "Why, sir, I do believe you're admitting you noticed my legs," she said with a flirtatious air.

"That and much more."

Warmed by his sincere compliment, she could only look at him with a broad smile on her face that faltered only a bit when Jess pulled up in front of a large, colonial-style house. It took him a few moments to find a parking space, since it appeared most of the guests had already arrived. He helped Sara out, then gave her his arm while she slipped her shoes back on.

"Why don't we go anywhere else but here?" she whispered, gripping his hand so hard he was convinced he had lost all feeling. "I'd even settle for a hot night at the bowling alley."

"It's just a party. Nothing can happen," he told her, guiding her up the walkway.

"At least Tess and Charlie are here." She gestured toward a dark blue Toyota with her free hand.

Sara stood slightly behind Jess as he rang the doorbell. She began to shrink back even more when a woman in her late fifties came to the door and smiled brightly at Jess.

"Pastor, I'm so glad you could come," she said warmly, opening the screen door.

"Thank you, Mrs. Marcy. I hope you don't mind that I brought a lady with me." He pulled Sara forward.

The woman's smile slipped. "Hello, Sara." Her greeting was far from warm.

Jess's own smile didn't waver as he pulled Sara into the house. Mrs. Marcy's manner continued to be a little forced as she introduced Jess to a few people he didn't know. As for Sara, her introduction was glossed over in a very slick manner.

"You're doing fine," he whispered in her ear when Mrs. Marcy was called away.

Her attention was diverted by a steely-eyed glare directed at her from across the room. Mrs. Masterson looked at her very slowly from head to toe as if she were something very distasteful.

When Jess looked down at Sara inquiringly, she raised her face, eyes very somber. "Then why do I feel as if I was a bastard attending a family picnic," she murmured, suddenly wishing she was anywhere but here.

"You're worrying about something that doesn't exist."

"Oh? Then take a look at Mrs. Masterson, because if looks could kill, I would be lying dead on this floor."

Jess glanced toward the older woman and saw what Sara meant. Mrs. Masterson's lips were compressed with anger, her eyes blazing with that same fury. Plastering a smile on his face, he walked directly toward her with a worried Sara in tow.

"Jess, no!" she hissed, vainly pulling against his firm grip.

"Mrs. Masterson, it's good to see you," he said cheerfully.

"Reverend," she said in a clipped tone, but her eyes were on Sara. "Aren't you afraid you made a grave mistake?"

He looked down at his clothing then around at the other men who were similarly clothed. "None that I can think of."

The older woman stared directly at Sara, eyeing her bare shoulders with patent disapproval, even though many women present wore either strapless or halter dresses that left a great deal more bare skin showing than hers did. "I don't believe I saw your name on Geraldine's invitation list."

"I didn't realize she had to have it approved first," Sara shot back, receiving a congratulatory squeeze of the hand from Jess.

Mrs. Masterson turned back to Jess. "We'll talk next week, Reverend." Sara privately thought she sounded exactly like the queen granting an audience to one of her subjects.

"Offhand I'm not sure what my schedule is, but I will let you know," Jess said easily. "Well, we must mingle." With a parting smile he guided Sara away. "That wasn't so bad, was it?" he murmured in her ear as they headed for Tess and Charlie, who were standing with another couple Sara knew.

She resisted the urge to laugh out loud with sheer happiness. "Just about as painless as having your tooth pulled by the string-on-the-doorknob method."

"You survived!" Tess hugged her tightly, whispering, "I saw the two of you talking to Old Stoneface. She looks like she's about ready to bust a garter."

"I don't think she would dare do it in public," Sara replied wryly.

Tess grinned. "See, you walked in, and the roof didn't fall down."

"You didn't see Mrs. Marcy's face when she saw who Jess brought with him."

"Forget Mrs. Marcy. Just guzzle the wine and eat the great food she's providing," she advised. "And be glad you're not the one who has to clean up."

And for a while Sara did relax and enjoy the party. She was grateful that Jess rarely left her side for more than a few minutes. Later on in the evening she noticed the buzzing among some of the older members of the party and the way they looked at her and at Jess, and it began to make her feel uncomfortable. Pretty soon her smile grew forced and her conversation stiff.

It didn't take Jess long to realize that Sara was no longer enjoying herself. Taking his time, he steered her through the people while saying their goodbyes. Some were friendly toward them, others were not. But Sara didn't expect miracles. By now she had a roaring headache and wanted nothing more than to take some aspirin and go to bed.

"Now do you understand why I rarely go out?" she said, as she climbed into the Bronco and laid her head back.

"The Creation took six days; why should you expect something that had been festering for fifteen years to disappear overnight?"

Sara didn't think it was funny and said so.

"Sara, I'm just proud of you for going with me tonight," he said quietly, reaching across the seat to grasp her hand. "But you're expecting too much from them too soon."

"Am I? What's wrong with people having good manners? Why should I go to a party where people are pretty much going to turn their backs on me?"

"No one turned their back on you," he insisted.

"Please." She drew the word out. "You saw Mrs. Marcy's expression when she saw me. You would have thought I was somebody's mutt with muddy paws from the way she treated me."

"You're overreacting."

Sara laughed bitterly. "Far from it. Now if you don't mind, I would just like to go home and take a bottle of aspirin for my headache." She looked out the window. "While I may not be the brightest person in the world, I do know that this is not the way to my house."

"No," Jess agreed. "But if we end up fighting tonight I wouldn't like the world to hear us." He continued driving out of town.

"I said I want to go home." Her voice was raised.

He shook his head. "Not until we settle a few things."

"What's wrong? Didn't I behave well enough for you?" Sara demanded to know. "Be careful what you say, or I might think that the only reason you took me there was to show the townspeople you could do anything you damn well please! Or perhaps infer that I'm your next project. My, wouldn't that look good on your record." Her voice turned dramatic. "Oh, yes, let's convert the town tramp, shall we?"

Jess's knuckles turned white. "I'm beginning to think you had too much wine at that party, Sara, because you're saying things you don't mean."

"Now you're implying I'm a drunk." She was so caught up in her misery she was beyond knowing what she was saying. "Just take me home, Jess. I don't have anything further to say to you."

His voice hardened. "Perhaps you don't, but I have quite a bit to say to you, and you will listen to me, Sara, whether you like it or not."

Chapter Twelve

Jess wasn't aware how long he drove. He just knew he wanted to get far enough away so that they wouldn't encounter anyone they knew who could cause Sara to withdraw. And he couldn't afford that when he intended to talk to Sara in a way he doubted she would appreciate. Forty minutes later he stopped at a fast-food restaurant for two cups of coffee and carried them out to Sara in the truck. Without a word he left again, heading for the drugstore across the street. When he returned, he tossed a small bottle of aspirin into her lap.

"Hope this is okay." He got in and switched on the engine. He drove down the street, hoping this town was like so many others where the park was situated in the middle of town. He breathed a silent sigh of relief when he saw one ahead of him. He pulled into the parking lot and stopped at one end.

Sara's head was tipped down in thought. "Thank you for the aspirin," she said finally.

"Now you have no reason to go home right away," he said in a clipped tone, taking his cup of coffee from her.

Sara sipped the hot brew gratefully. With that and the two aspirin she had taken she began to feel better. If they could sit there in silence, she knew she would be fine, but she should have known that Jess wouldn't allow that to happen.

Jess finished his coffee, replaced the lid and tossed the cup into a small, plastic trash bag in the back.

"I'm telling you this here, because there are some things that are said better in the dark where we can't see each other's face. Actually my face," he said sardonically. "And this is one of those subjects."

Sara frowned. What was he talking about?

He stared out over the steering wheel, across the darkened park toward the brightly lit playground. "The reason you couldn't find me when Tim was born was because I was in jail." He didn't react when he heard her gasp. He couldn't allow himself to look at her if he wanted to finish his story.

"Oh, Jess," she whispered, touching his arm.

"Sara, please don't say anything more until I've finished my story," he begged. "It's going to be difficult enough to talk about."

She sat back, giving him all the space he needed and remained silent. Of all the reasons that had run through her head when she had tried to contact him, his being in jail hadn't been one of them, even considering that he was known for his wild nature and affinity for getting into trouble.

Jess looked down at his hands curved over the steering wheel. Hands that had gotten him into more trouble than he had ever counted on.

"I felt pretty torn up when you left me." He smiled wryly. "Oh, I know I acted like the prize ass of all time. It was natural you wanted to get married, that certainly would have been the next step with the way we were going. After all, we were practically living together."

"I was so wrong," she said softly, cradling her coffee cup between her hands for warmth; but the kind of warmth she needed was more emotional than physical. "I grew afraid you were getting tired of me, and I started feeling possessive of you. I wanted to be with you all the time, and I worried every time we were apart. I was afraid you'd find someone else."

He shook his head. "No, it wasn't just that. Oh, I admit that I felt suffocated at times, but it had more to do than just with you. It was me, too. I wanted so much for us, and I didn't know where to get it. I was bored with school and didn't think I'd learn anything there. You wanted me with you all the time, and I felt the need to get out and find something that would fulfill me. When you told me you wanted us to get married, I panicked. I had no prospects, the job I had at that printing shop barely gave me enough for expenses, and your waitressing job was no better. I was twenty-two, I saw my life ahead of me, and while deep down I loved and wanted to marry you, the shallow part of me wanted to see what else I could find. I felt we were too young, and that was all I could think to tell you when you started talking about marriage."

"While I saw it as the all-time brush-off."

Jess turned in the seat to face her. "I didn't think you'd leave me so abruptly and without any word."

She offered a tiny smile. "I was afraid if I didn't pack up my pride and leave right away, I wouldn't leave at all. And if I stayed, I would always have the fear you would leave me. In my naïveté I was convinced marriage was the only way I could hold you."

Both were lost in their own painful memories.

"At first I told myself you were off somewhere pouting and would come around. Then a week passed, a second week passed, and pretty soon I knew you weren't coming back.'' He spoke in a detached tone as if talking about two other people. ''When that happened, I went on an all-time drinking binge. I called you lots of names, most of them not pretty and definitely not repeatable. I said I was better off without you and I was going to live my life to the fullest.'' He looked at her, ashamed of the person he had once been, but knowing he had to tell her all of it. ''There were other girls, I won't deny it, but every time I felt empty, and then I felt even angrier at you. I lost my job, I hadn't attended classes in weeks, and pretty soon all the anger that had built up inside of me exploded. I picked a fight with someone in a bar for no reason at all. He landed in the hospital with multiple injuries, and I landed in jail. It turned out the guy had some connections with the law, so I was slapped with a trumped-up charge and given nine months for assault and battery.''

Sara blinked rapidly to keep the tears back, but they still continued to flow down her cheeks. ''I shouldn't have left,'' she sobbed. ''This wouldn't have happened if I had stayed with you.''

''No,'' he argued, grabbing her hands and holding them tightly. ''Sara, it could have happened later on for all we know. I suffered from a lot of internal pressure then. Pressure I had put on myself, just the way Tim puts it on himself. I had a horrible temper, and I needed an outlet. It was unfortunate that somebody had to be hurt in the process, but in the long run it was the best thing that could have happened to me.''

''Best? You were jailed, probably treated like I don't know what, just because someone wanted you to suffer more than you should have.'' She shook her head, wanting the story not to be true, but knowing he wouldn't lie to her. Not about this.

"Sara, I was meant to be in that jail, because it was there I met the man who turned my life around," Jess explained to her. "Wayne was the jail's chaplain, and he refused to allow me to feel sorry for myself. As for my macho act, he saw through that right away. If it hadn't been for him, I would have sat there for those nine months feeling bitter and probably scheming to get even with the world for putting me there. Instead, Wayne taught me how to deal with my feelings, he forced me to talk out my anger and showed me how to turn it around to my benefit." He smiled, remembering the man who had done so much for him. "He kept me sane and whole, Sara. And when I got out of jail, Wayne let me stay with him until I decided what I wanted to do with my life."

"And you chose to become a minister," she murmured, stunned by the turn of events in his life that were just as traumatic as her own had been.

He nodded. "I thought about it and prayed long and hard before I made my decision. Then I went to Wayne, and we talked and prayed more. I knew it would be a hard pull, because my grades weren't exactly the best to begin with, but I worked two jobs to pay my expenses and eventually qualified for a scholarship. I knew I wanted to obtain an additional degree in psychology, because I wanted to help troubled kids. Surprisingly I graduated from school with honors and began my work in a halfway house with Wayne. Sara." He silently urged her to look at him. "For the first time I was at peace with myself and doing what I wanted with my life. I guess you could say I found my niche."

She nodded. "I'm glad you found what you were looking for, Jess," she whispered. "And thank you for trusting me enough to tell me your story. I'm afraid I feel very tired. Would you mind taking me home now?"

Jess stared at her for a moment, but she refused to look at him. "All right," he said finally, turning back to switch on the engine.

Sara didn't say a word during the trip back to her house. When Jess parked in front, she picked up her shoes and purse from the floor.

"Obviously you never told Tim your story," she commented softly.

"No, although I have thought about it."

"I think you should." She placed her hand on the door handle. "You answered a lot of questions for me tonight, Jess. I'm grateful to know that our parting wasn't all my fault as I had thought for a long time. I'm also glad you're finally at peace with yourself." Her eyes shimmered with tears, but she refused to allow them to fall. "I only wish I could have given you that peace, but I guess my love for you hadn't been enough. Good night, Jess."

Before he could move or say a word, she was out of the truck and running down the walkway to the front door, where a porch light shone invitingly. She didn't look back as she slipped inside. The porch went dark, and Jess still sat inside the truck. Whatever reaction he might have expected from Sara, hurt feelings wasn't a part of it. And this time he knew it had nothing to do with injured pride. She honestly believed her love hadn't been enough for him! That wasn't true, but how did he explain it to her?

The truck moved slowly away from the house. Jess was aware someone watched him from behind the living-room drapes. He wasn't eager to go home just now, but he didn't know what else to do. He entered his empty house and wandered through the rooms that were kept clean and orderly thanks to Mrs. Harris, but they still had no personality. The woman was a wonder with a vacuum and dust rag, but fresh flowers never graced the vases, because she said the petals dropped almost right away and cluttered the tables and too many knickknacks were dust collectors. He remembered seeing the wildflowers in a simple glass vase on Sara's dining-room table and a collection of pewter figurines in a tall glass case in one corner of the den. They didn't look like dust collectors, merely something the owner enjoyed. Nothing there was expensive, just well cared for as if each tiny item carried a special memory.

He went into his bedroom and looked around the spare furnishings; a double bed with a cream-colored bedspread, a dresser, an easy chair in one corner with a reading lamp behind it, nothing fancy just plain furniture that carried no stories for him, held no memories. He had kept few personal items that meant anything to him, because theft happened in the halfway house. No matter how much they tried to help some of the kids, they still didn't know how to do anything else but steal.

He was still glad he told Sara what had happened years ago. It wasn't a pretty story, but he knew it had to be told. Maybe she could understand why he hadn't gone after her then. Actually it had taken the decision out of his hands, because to this day he wondered if he would have tried to find her or just written her off as a great affair that was meant to end the way it had.

Still, he thought about the softness of her hair, the floral fragrance of her skin and her response when he kissed her. Oh, yes, the response. That was more than a surprise. That was something to cherish. And if he played his cards right and took great care, he could have even more to cherish than the memories of a few kisses and the feel of a woman's body under his hands. Until then he would have to concentrate on his own work and pray everything would turn out all right.

SARA CREPT DOWN THE HALL, went into her room and slowly undressed, leaving her clothes scattered across the carpet. She sat on the bed, her back braced against the headboard, her chin resting on her drawn-up knees. Now that Jess had answered so many of her questions about what had happened after they had parted, she found she had even more to ask him.

His story was an earth-shattering revelation to her. The last thing she had expected to hear was that he had spent time in jail or that a minister had turned his life around. She realized her feelings were a little selfish, because she had once believed she was all he needed to be happy. Now she had learned differently, and she would be a fool if she didn't admit it hurt.

She began to wonder if anything would make sense now. The two sides of Jess—the wild and free lover and the minister—couldn't be reconciled. Could she expect them to? If she was smart enough, she'd say no. So which man was she interested in? The man she once knew or the man she now knew? That wasn't an easy question to answer. It was a long time before she could relax enough to slip under the covers and try to sleep.

TIM SAT in the dark living room listening to his mother's bedtime preparations. She was in such a state when she arrived home that she hadn't even noticed his presence in the front room. But Tim noticed her, and how upset she seemed. It was his guess that the reverend had something to do with it. He could feel his temper beginning to rise, and he got up from his chair, determined to seek out the man and find out what he had said to upset his mother. But caution intervened. He knew if he did, his mother would never forgive him, and he would only end up in more trouble. Besides, his brain whispered, what if it didn't have to do with the preacher at all, what if someone at the party had said something rude to her?

That didn't stop him from wanting the answers behind his mother's sorrow. No matter what, there was something going on between his mother and the preacher. He could feel it. He just wasn't sure it was right. He stayed in the chair for a long time trying to figure out the vagaries of the adult population.

By UNSPOKEN CONSENT, Tim and Jackson ignored Sara's quiet manner the next day. Tim took off for his job at the hardware store and Jackson for the station. The older man suggested to Sara that she come down after lunch, since she had had a late night.

"You haven't asked me one question about the party." She thought she would bring it up first, before he caught her off guard as he so enjoyed doing.

"You want to tell me about it, you will. You don't want to, you won't," Jackson drawled. "I ain't gonna push."

Sara rolled her eyes. "Jackson, this is not you, so don't try to be some endearing old man when we all know what a rascal you really are." She wrinkled her nose at his wide grin. "I do admit it was an experience. Mrs. Masterson wasn't pleased to see me, but she managed to keep her claws to herself. The food was very good, quite a few people I knew were there, and whether I wanted to admit it or not, I did have fun. At least in the beginning.''

"Until someone insulted you?''

Sara shrugged. "Not exactly. Oh, a few people turned their backs on me, which didn't surprise me, but there was nothing out in the open that I could battle, which was probably just as well.''

"So why aren't you happy about it?'' he asked bluntly.

She shook her head. "Because of other things I'd really rather not go into just now.''

Jackson's bushy brows drew together in an intimidating frown. "Dammit, I didn't want to see you hurt, and he's gone and done it already! Maybe I should go over there and have a talk with him. You're just white-washing the facts, aren't you?''

"No, it's not what you think,'' Sara protested swiftly, afraid the feisty old man would march over to Jess's house and confront him. She knew that would be a scene she would never be able to live down, even though she loved him dearly for wanting to defend her in the best way he knew how.

He didn't look convinced, but he finally went down to the station, leaving Sara alone with her thoughts—a state she wasn't happy with since she had been doing too much thinking since she had left Jess last night.

She poured herself a cup of coffee and curled up in an easy chair in the den, again going over her new feelings for Jess, the events of last night, his story. That was when it hit her.

He didn't have to have told her. He could have kept it quiet, and she would have been none the wiser. He certainly wouldn't have lied to her if she had insisted on knowing what had happened to him back then, but he still could have gotten around it.

She told herself she would have to call him. But not just yet. She still wanted to get all of this sorted out in her mind before talking to him. And the best way to do that was retire to the kitchen and whip up a chocolate-chip cheesecake.

TIM STOPPED BY Jess's house after work, as per Jess's request, and with the athletic clothing he had suggested.

"What are we doing?" Tim demanded, when Jess met him at the front door, wearing navy jogging shorts and a white T-shirt. "Hey, I do enough running in school, I don't want to do it on the weekends."

"The time has come for you to learn how to work off some of that frustration you build up," he replied, tossing his keys up and down in his hand. "Come on."

"Where are we going?" He followed Jess down the driveway to the Bronco.

"The best place to learn," he said mysteriously, as they drove down the street.

Their destination turned out to be the YMCA, where Jess steered Tim to the locker room to change, then led him into the weight room. For the next hour he instructed the boy in the proper use of the weights and set up a training program for him.

"We're going to be coming here three times a week for a while," Jess told him, after they had finished their session.

"If you expect me to jump up and down for joy, you're going to wait a long time," Tim muttered, climbing slowly into the Bronco and feeling the pull of each sore muscle.

Jess stopped at a McDonald's, and they sat in a corner table drinking Cokes and talking. What Jess tried to do was get Tim to discuss his thoughts about school and the people he interrelated with. The more he heard, the more he understood the boy.

After sitting so long at McDonald's and then climbing back into the truck, Tim found out exactly how stiff his body was. "No wonder you don't have a temper, you probably killed it if this is how you work off your inner frustrations," he grumbled, when Jess stopped the truck in front of Tim's house.

"The first time is always the worst," Jess replied. "Don't worry, you'll find that it gets easier every time. Just give it time. A hot bath will help keep your muscles from stiffening up too much. I'll see you Monday."

"What happened to you?" Sara asked, watching her son limp through the kitchen.

"He's trying to kill me," he muttered, groaning when he tried to lift his arm. "I swear he wants to see how long it will take before he breaks every bone in my body."

"What do you mean?" she asked, alarmed and suddenly fearing the worst.

Tim shook his head. "His idea of working out frustration is to go to the Y. And we did just that—work out."

Sara smiled. "And you're feeling a bit stiff. Don't worry, dinner will be ready in about twenty minutes. You'll feel better after you eat."

"I'm not so sure I'm hungry," he muttered, leaving the kitchen. "I'm going to take another hot shower."

"A hot bath would help you more," she called after him.

"Yeah, that's what he said." Tim limped along to his room. It wasn't until he was standing under the shower that he realized he hadn't asked Reverend Larkin the question he wanted to: what had happened last night to make his mother cry? He filed that thought away, because he wasn't about to be sidetracked Monday afternoon.

He groaned when he tried to bend over in the shower. He groaned again when he struggled to sit down in the kitchen chair for dinner, and while he watched television he merely stretched out on the carpet, saying it was easier.

Sara watched her disgruntled son and hid her smile. Apparently he wasn't too pleased with Jess's idea of easing various frustrations. A devilish thought hit her as she wondered if that was his way to take care of sexual frustration, too. She couldn't believe he hadn't been tempted over the years, and a minister's life was so high profile that he certainly couldn't have an affair and have it go unnoticed.

Around ten o'clock Sara announced she was going to read for a while and have an early night. Instead, the moment her bedroom door was closed she picked up her phone and dialed Jess's number.

"It's me," she said unnecessarily when he answered. "I'm not calling too late, am I?"

"No." His voice was equally soft. "Although I will admit I'm surprised to hear from you."

Sara jumped in before she could lose her nerve. "Jess, from the beginning I always wondered what happened to you, and then when I find out I back off. I know this sounds foolish, but it was a shock to me."

"That's understandable."

"You're not the same man I remembered," she explained. "While we were together you never went out and broke the law just for the hell of it— Sorry about that," she murmured apologetically. "But you did take chances back then. Chances that could have landed you in a great deal of trouble, but you never cared. Chances you wouldn't even consider now, and I don't think it all has to do with maturity, either."

Jess didn't have to ask for clarification. It was so incredibly easy to understand. She didn't see him as the same man. Luckily that was something he could easily remedy.

"Let's have a picnic lunch Monday at one," he suggested. "We can talk then."

She shouldn't leave the station, because she had already taken so much time off, but she knew it had to be done. "All right. In fact I'll fix the food, and you won't need to bring a thing but yourself. Good night, Jess."

"Good night, Sara."

JESS'S MANNER TOWARD HER Sunday morning was the same as his manner toward every other member of the congregation. He smiled, shook her hand and wished her a good week. When she looked up at him for a brief second, she could have sworn she saw a flash of that old Larkin devilment in his eyes, but it was gone so quickly she wondered if she could have imagined it. By Monday afternoon when it was time to meet Jess at the lake, she was convinced she had imagined that expression in his eyes.

She packed the wicker basket with all sorts of goodies made for tempting a man. Just in case she hadn't imagined that wicked twinkle in his eye, she dressed with the same idea in mind.

As before, Jess was sitting on the large rock. He wore faded jeans that clung to his body like a second skin, a white T-shirt, and dusty, brown boots. Sara slid out of her car and stood there staring at the man seated on the boulder at the water's edge. For a moment she was taken back in time. She slowly turned and pulled the basket and a heavy blanket from the back seat.

"I brought lunch," she called out, holding the basket up.

He smiled, and the smile conveyed that he liked what he saw. Who wouldn't? Sara wore a pair of blue chambray shorts that hugged her hips and a matching, tailored shirt with the tails tied just under her breasts leaving a pale gold expanse of bare skin for his hungry eyes to feast on. He watched her walk toward him, unable to keep his eyes off the heavenly sight before him.

"What did you bring for dessert?"

Sara froze for a second, unable to believe her ears. "Chocolate-chip cheesecake," she said finally. "I promised you some the last time we were here."

He hopped down from the boulder, taking the blanket out of her hand and spreading it over the bare area, then sat down in the center. He held his hand up in a silent offer to help her down.

"Do you and Tim go to the Y again today?" she asked, using any subject she could think of.

He grinned. "Think he'll be able to handle it?"

Sara couldn't help grinning back. "I don't know. He was moaning and groaning like an old man Saturday night. Jackson said Tim sounded worse than he did when his rheumatism was acting up. You wore him out so much he didn't even feel like going out with his friends. And for him to miss a Saturday night out says a lot. I understand what you're doing, and I think it's wonderful," she said huskily.

"If he had tried out for school sports, he would have been better off." Jess stared into her eyes, noticing they had been highlighted with a touch of gray shadow and blue liner. "I know you kept him working at the station, but that was only when you could get him there. Since he doesn't consider it a real job, he didn't always show up when you needed him."

"Doesn't consider it a real job?" Sara was incredulous. "I pay him a decent hourly wage, I don't set rigid hours for him, but before he started working at the hardware store I did expect him to help out at the station certain days after school and on weekends."

Jess held up his hand. "That's the key word—help. You expected him to 'help out,' not to work per se. He wasn't an employee, he was the owner's son, who worked in the station when she needed him."

"I understand what you're saying, but that doesn't mean I like it."

Sara carefully unpacked the basket and set the food out, fried chicken, fruit salad, yeasty homemade rolls with golden honey accompanying them, iced tea and several large slices of her cheesecake.

"I'd say this required quite a bit of preparation," Jess hazarded a guess, slathering honey on a roll, then placing several pieces of chicken on his paper plate.

"Jackson has been asking for fried chicken for a long time, so I decided this was as good a time as any to fix it," she lied, concentrating on her fruit salad.

He grasped her chin and tilted her face upward. "You never could lie, Sara," he said gently, his thumb rubbing the corner of her mouth with seductive pressure. He held out his roll, inviting her to take a bite. Keeping her eyes on his, she opened her mouth and bit into the still-warm roll. A drop of honey glistened on her bottom lip, and before she could wipe it off he did it for her with his tongue.

Sara's breath caught, leaving a heaviness in her chest. She inhaled the warm scent of male skin and aftershave. He was so close to her she could see the pores of his skin and a tiny nick where he had cut himself shaving that morning. She felt as giddy as if she had drunk champagne. Before she could lean further into his half embrace, he moved away.

"Now let's try this chicken," he said matter-of-factly, holding a piece of white meat against her lips. Again her lips opened, and she bit into the juicy meat. From then on Sara didn't lift a finger to feed herself as Jess continued to tempt her with succulent bites of chicken, the choicest bits of fruit and rolls. When they finished every bite, he used a plastic fork to slice bites of cheesecake and fed that to her.

Sara couldn't keep her eyes off him as her brain raced with questions regarding this new mood. Correction, not a new mood. This was the Jess she had first met and fallen in love with. Her blue eyes wide, she watched him pick up a napkin and dab the corners of her mouth. The closer he got, the more convinced she was he was going to kiss her.

"There, all nice and clean." Jess smiled at her.

He continued smiling as his face again grew closer to hers. "Let's see if you taste as good without honey as you did with," he murmured against her lips.

"The chicken," she breathed, fully aware every piece she had brought had been picked clean, but there was no real protest in her voice or eyes.

"He'll have to find his own lady to kiss." Jess leaned forward until Sara had no choice but to lay back against the blanket, her hair fanning out around her head in golden waves. "I'm glad to see you wore it loose," he murmured, touching one strand, watching it curl around his fingers.

"Should we?" she questioned tentatively. Now that she had accomplished what she had cooked and dressed for, she wasn't sure it was a good idea after all. Her apprehension disappeared the moment he stretched out beside her on his stomach.

"Oh, yes." His mouth played lightly over hers, sipping and nibbling until her lips opened, inviting his exploration. His tongue slid over her lower lip then along the bowed contours of her upper lip before slowly slipping inside. The moist warmth and sweet taste was more than he remembered. Groaning, his mouth covered hers fully, and his tongue thrust deep inside.

Sara's heart didn't stop singing. This was the Jess she remembered. The hard, lean man kissing her with a voracious hunger was the same man who had made the fierce love to her that resulted in their son. She curled her arms around his shoulders pulling him even closer to her. Husky murmurs were traded between the two lovers as their mouths reacquainted themselves with every centimeter of their faces and throats. Needing more, Sara eagerly pulled Jess's T-shirt away from his jeans and slid her hands underneath to stroke her palms over his heated skin.

"Sara, you feel the same yet different," he murmured.

"I am different." She adored the feel of his body over hers. She arched up against him in what she hoped was a seductive manner. Finally she took his hand and laid it over her breast.

It could have been minutes or even hours as they lay together, their lips meeting again and again, their bodies rolling gently together, their mouths exchanging soft love words interspersed with gentle laughter. Their eyes met in another silent form of language. They became aware of nothing but each other, until Sara knew she wanted nothing more than for Jess to make love to her and said so.

After she spoke he closed his eyes tightly and rolled away, keeping his arm crooked over his eyes. Sara lay there, confused by the sudden turn of events. One thing she hadn't expected was to be rejected so abruptly. She lay on the blanket breathing deeply to dispel the tumultuous feelings running through her throbbing body.

"Did—did I do something wrong?" she asked hesitantly, her voice raw with unshed tears.

He turned his head and offered her a slow smile. "No, love, you did everything right. That's the problem."

Sara sat up on her knees. "What's the problem?"

Jess sighed wearily. "The problem is this is not the right time for us when there's so much else going on. And when I do make love to you, I will make love to you as my wife, no less."

Sara could only stare at him, certain she had misunderstood him and unsure if she wanted to believe what she had heard.

Chapter Thirteen

"As your wife?" Sara echoed, then threw back her head, laughing so hard Jess wasn't sure if she found it that funny or she was hysterical. He decided to opt for the former.

"I don't see the humor in it," he said stiffly.

Just as abruptly her laughter stopped. She took several deep breaths and organized her thoughts before speaking. "Jess, right now we have no solid ground to discuss something as serious as marriage. There is definitely a physical attraction between us, one that started years ago and has redeveloped now. But that isn't something to base a long-term commitment on." Her eyes looked very sad and much older than her years.

"Jess, we share a son, and I would never deny that, although it still isn't something to bring out into the open just now. As I told you before, this town has rigid ideas. While many understand the world has changed and unwed mothers aren't to be ostracized anymore, they still wouldn't understand if they learned their new minister, the one they've come to respect so highly, fathered a child sixteen years ago and that child is known as a troublemaker."

"I was not a saint back then," he said tightly.

"None of us were. But Jess, what you're trying to do is make up for the past, and I can't allow you to do that."

Jess stood up and walked down to the water's edge. With his body rigid and hands braced on his hips, he looked like a man carrying the weight of the world on his shoulders.

"I'm neither a martyr nor a small boy who doesn't know his own mind, Sara," he gritted. "I've thought about us for a long time. We had our problems in the past, but they no longer exist. I want us to start a new life together."

"It's not that easy."

"Oh? Why not?" he shot back, then attacked further when he saw she had no answer. "It's not easy only to you, no one else. You're just afraid."

"And what's wrong with that? Your work is very important to you and others." Knowing the kind of man he had grown into, Sara was aware the problems people showered him with, the way they looked up to him. No matter was so trivial they didn't feel comfortable enough to talk to the pastor about. There were some who would ridicule him if they knew the truth about Tim. She couldn't allow that. It was in that split second that Sara knew she had only one option. And no matter what, she couldn't discuss it with Jess. No, this was something she had to do on her own. For years she had kept her own counsel, worked hard to provide a decent home for her son and to try to keep him out of trouble, yet the minute Jess arrived in town she ran to him with every minor problem. That was also the moment that she knew she loved him all over again, and this time her love was that of a mature woman for a mature man.

"Jess, I have to return to the station," she said quietly, repacking the basket.

He nodded, not bothering to turn around. He was still so angry with her he couldn't think straight. "Just tell me one thing."

Sara was instantly wary. "If I can."

"This wasn't some kind of lark for you, was it? I mean, we did part on pretty bad terms the last time. You didn't look at it as some kind of revenge, did you?"

She could feel her eyes fill with tears, but she wasn't about to allow them to fall. "No, I didn't." She carried the basket to her car and turned back to look at him. He still hadn't turned around. Without thinking she went to him and laced her arms around his waist; she pressed her lips against the warm cotton of his shirt. "Back then and now you were the best thing to happen to me," she whispered. Just as suddenly her arms dropped, and she ran back to her car.

Jess didn't turn when he heard her car leaving. Funny, he thought to himself, he would have sworn that she had said goodbye to him. Not a goodbye, see you later, but a very final goodbye.

He did love her. The warm, all-encompassing love between two adults. He wanted to make love to her, he wanted to explore her body and rediscover what he had once known and learn the changes that had been made over the years. He couldn't miss the fuller breasts and womanly curve of her hips that hadn't been there before. The physical side of his love was very strong, but this time he wanted to take the time to talk to her, to learn her thoughts and views on everything that he hadn't bothered about before, because all he had thought about was taking her to bed. It took him a lot of years, but he finally understood what true love was. And he wanted to share it with Sara.

He was tempted to tell all to Tim, but he had promised Sara that wouldn't be done until they both decided the time was right. She had asked that he tell the boy about his time in jail, and he would keep that promise that very afternoon. He remained by the water for a long time looking at the placid surface as if he could find all his answers there. If only it was that easy.

JACKSON WATCHED SARA CLOSELY, noting she had almost dropped a crescent wrench on her foot several times.

"You gonna tell me what's got you in a snit?" he rumbled, stopping her from using the wrong oil filter in the car she was working on.

"I'm not in a snit," she said quietly.

"Then what do you call it?"

Sara shrugged. What would she call it? Jess thought her reaction to his offhand proposal meant she viewed his words as a joke. Far from it. If she hadn't laughed, she quite probably would have broken down in tears. "Call it a wish to return to simpler times."

"There never was anything like that, honey," Jackson said gruffly, laying a grimy hand on her shoulder and giving it a squeeze. "Don't ask for somethin' you can't have."

This time she almost didn't hold back her tears. She was well aware that just because the man was in his seventies didn't mean he was in his dotage. He was too shrewd at times.

"I could have had it," she whispered, staring off into space. "I could have." She was so lost in her thoughts that she didn't hear the old man move away.

WHEN TIM SHOWED UP that afternoon, he and Jess first drove over to the Y for their workout. Tim still found it a chore, and even with the assurances from Jess and the man in charge of the gym that the more times he worked at it the easier it would become, he still loudly complained he was ready to die. What he didn't admit was that deep down he was already beginning to enjoy working with the free weights and discovering just how much body strength he had. Not the kind of strength to use in a fight, but the kind that utilized his entire body and mind. When he finished, streams of sweat flowed down his body, but he felt more relaxed than he had in a long time.

"What does the judge think of you counseling me like this instead of sessions in an office where I tell you how much I hate everybody?" Tim asked when they stopped for a Coke.

Jess laughed. "You've watched too many movies. When I worked at the halfway house, I shot baskets with one kid and jogged with another." He went on to talk about some of the boys he worked with, being careful to keep personal information confidential but giving Tim an idea exactly what he had done in Atlanta. "My methods are considered unorthodox by quite a few people, but I feel we then have something in common and interact better for it. I admit it didn't always work, but I didn't fail every time, either. Judge Carmody doesn't believe in too much; I think he was born a cynic. But I do know he contacted everybody possible about me and learned enough to allow me to handle this my way. If I screw up, well, I'll probably be in chains right next to you." He grinned, receiving a grin back that perfectly echoed his own.

"Nah, I doubt that would happen to you," Tim scoffed.

"It did once."

Tim put his Coke down and looked at the older man. "You were in chains once?" He took it as a joke, but the serious expression on Jess's face told him differently.

"No, I was in jail."

Tim laughed hesitantly. "What happened, did you protect one of those kids you counseled or something?"

"No, I was in jail for nine months for picking a fight and beating up a kid pretty badly," Jess said quietly.

That caught the boy's attention. "For fighting? Hey, you're one of the most laid-back guys I've ever met. No offense, but I can't see you doing that."

Jess nodded. "I did, Tim. There was a time when my temper was as bad, if not worse than yours. When I grew angry I used to go out just looking for a fight, and due to the places I frequented it wasn't very difficult to find one." He kept eye contact with him, determined he was going to believe a story he told few people. In fact, Sara had been the first to hear it in years.

"Why?" Tim asked. "Why would you fight with a guy and land in jail?"

"Because the girl I thought I loved then had left me," he said quietly. "I was twenty-two, cocky as all get-out and had the love of a beautiful girl. She wanted to get married, I didn't. In the end she left me, and my ego insisted she would be back. She never returned, and I grew angrier with each passing day. Pretty soon I convinced myself I didn't need her and began partying pretty hard. One night I got drunk, felt a little maudlin because she had left me and picked on some kid who was probably half my size. The fight wasn't pretty, the judge said I was guilty and I was clapped in jail before I knew it."

"You did all that for some girl?" He was incredulous. "Hey, it's not worth it. There's others out there." Tim stopped at the knowing look on Jess's face, then flashed a sheepish smile. "It sounds like something I should listen to, huh?"

"You're still young, but that's your only excuse." He clapped him on the back. "Still, it's not a piece of bad advice, and if I were you, I'd try to remember it in the future."

Tim grimaced. "I've already decided girls aren't worth the trouble."

"Sure, they are. And you'll agree when you find the right one," Jess said easily, tossing his empty cup in the trash. "I better get you back before your mother shoots me."

"I don't think she'd do that." Tim was unconcerned. "She really likes you." He stopped, his head bent as he fumbled for the proper words. "I was up when she came home from that party you took her to and, well, she was crying." He looked up, eyeing Jess. "No matter what some of the people said to her, even that old biddy Masterson, she never cried." His meaning came through loud and clear.

"No one was rude to her, Tim," Jess replied. "In fact, I think she enjoyed herself more than she expected. As to why she was crying, well, I told her the same story I told you," he said truthfully. "She took it rather hard. Not that she held anything against me, because she understood that was part of my past, not my present, but...well, women are notoriously softhearted." There was so much more he wanted to tell him. The problem was how to do it.

Tim thought about it. "Yeah, I guess it was a surprise for her. Some people around here treat her like dirt while they really aren't any better."

"That's why we're told to turn the other cheek," Jess told him. "And Sara has done an admirable job of doing just that. There aren't many women who could have stood up to what she has." He put the truck in gear and eased it out of its parking space. "Just remember she's suffered just as much as you say you have, and maybe the next time someone ticks you off you'll stop to think before you lash out."

"I won't make any promises," Tim warned. "I have a bad habit of not stopping to think."

"We all did it at one time or another. Just try, okay?" Jess advised. "That's all I ask."

Tim nodded. He looked out as the truck stopped in front of his house. He placed his hand on the door handle and paused. "I know you didn't have to do this," he said hesitantly. "Well, I just want you to know I appreciate it."

"I'm glad," he said quietly, watching him scramble out and lope toward the front door. Jess watched for a moment, hoping for a glimpse of Sara, but his luck ran out. He put the truck into gear and drove slowly down the road. One thing he had learned was that Tim was growing up faster than he or Sara realized. He only hoped that Tim would take the news of his parentage as well as he took the news of Jess's past. Too bad he couldn't feel as positive about it as he should.

SARA FELT STUNNED as she watched Tim help her with the dinner preparations, set the table and, after their meal, clear the table without any direction from her.

"Are you setting me up for something?" she asked as he dried the dishes while she washed. "Did you flunk a test? Do I have to show up for a parent-teacher conference tomorrow?"

"Set you up?" he laughed. "No, Mom, I just thought I'd surprise you by helping without you yelling at me to."

"I do not yell at you."

"Okay, but you do talk loud." He finished drying the last pan, and he carefully folded the towel and draped it over the rack. He slowly turned and leaned back against the counter. "Mom, Pastor Jess told me about his being in jail."

Her movements stilled. "He did?"

"He also told me that he had told you about it last Friday night. You see, I heard you come in the house crying, and I was afraid he had something to do with it," he confessed.

"Tim, you didn't start a fight with him, did you?" She automatically feared the worst.

He rolled his eyes, signifying that mothers seemed to refuse to believe their children could do something right for once. "Are you kidding? After what he told me, no one in their right mind would want to push him into fighting back unless they wanted some broken bones. The guy knows what he's talking about when it comes to bad tempers."

Sara finished wiping off the stove and counters before answering. "Then you understand the need to keep your temper under control," she said softly.

"Let me tell you, after he puts a guy through that workout you have no energy left to do anything," he admitted. "He and Ray, the guy in charge of the gym, keep telling me I'll get used to it, but I'll believe it when I see it."

Sara's lips quivered. Her little boy was growing up. She knew she was imagining it, but she could swear his body looked a bit broader and he acted more like an adult than a boy bordering on manhood. She crossed the room and threw her arms around him.

"Mom, you're not going to cry and get all female on me, are you?" He still wasn't used to dealing with women's changes of mood.

"No." She sniffed, then immediately felt like crying when she realized she couldn't put her arms all the way around him. "I guess I'm just discovering that before I know it you'll be leaving home. And Jackson won't have anyone to play poker with."

Tim patted her back awkwardly, not knowing what else to do. "Now you are getting all female on me," he accused. "Look, I'm not even sixteen yet, and you're already throwing me out of the house." He grinned, in hopes of teasing her out of her mood. "Maybe you should take up with the preacher. If nothing else, it would give the town something to talk about. Mom?" He wondered what made her turn pale. "Hey, I was only kidding. And it's not as if he sees you the way others do. He thinks you're really nice."

Sara turned away, resisting the urge to clench her fists at her sides. "I think he's a nice man, too," she said in a low voice. "And I'm sure he'll eventually find a nice woman to help him with his work." She forced herself to smile. "Now just because you helped me doesn't mean you get out of doing your homework. I want you to get to work in the next five minutes.''

Tim nodded, but he still puzzled over her sudden mood twist as he went to his room to do his homework.

JESS WAS GLAD for a quiet evening at home. Too many evenings were spent visiting members of his congregation or preparing for one of the three Bible study meetings he presided over or other various duties of a pastor. He decided it was the perfect time to catch up on some pleasure reading and had just settled down with a book when someone knocked on his door. Hoping it was Sara, he was surprised to find Cora Masterson on his doorstep.

''Mrs. Masterson, this is a surprise. Won't you come in?'' He stood back so she could enter. ''Would you care for some coffee?''

She walked stiff-backed into the living room and sat down, her back as properly aligned as it was when she walked. ''This is not a social call, Reverend.'' Her voice was cool as ice.

Jess took a chair, feeling as if he were the visitor in his own home. ''Oh?'' He sat back, waiting for her to come to her reason. He doubted he would have to wait long. He was right.

''I understand there aren't a great many eligible women in Henderson, Reverend,'' Mrs. Masterson said. ''And while that Murdock woman isn't married, she still isn't a proper companion for someone of your status.''

His stomach muscles clenched. ''My status?''

She nodded imperiously. "Of course, you have an impeccable reputation to maintain and being seen with a woman like her doesn't enhance it."

Jess's eyes darkened to a frosty shade. "What exactly do you mean by a woman like her?"

"After all, she does have a son and no husband." Mrs. Masterson talked as if she expected him to listen to her word as if it were law. "And if a woman has fallen once, it is expected she would fall again and this time drag an innocent man down with her." Her smile was cold. "It hasn't escaped some people's notice that your car is seen near the lake a great deal. And that her car has been seen driving in that direction at the same time."

"Really?" He glanced down at the carpet for a moment so he could compose his thoughts. When he did speak, his voice was so cold it should have frozen the woman sitting across from him, but he had a feeling her blood was already well below the freezing point. "Mrs. Masterson, from what I've heard, Sara had fallen in love with a man years ago, bore his child with no help from anyone save two old men who took her in and cared for her. When she inherited property many of the so-called good people of this town did nothing but malign her. In spite of it she raised her son, ran her business and did nothing to antagonize anyone, yet you persist in calling her names she doesn't deserve. Why?"

The older woman straightened up even more than usual before she stood up. "There is nothing personal in our feelings about the woman. But she is a bad example to our own young girls."

"Do you know how many girls have become pregnant in the past fifteen years?" he asked slyly.

Mrs. Masterson looked as if she couldn't believe he would dare question her judgment. "How many? I have no idea."

"I do." He smiled, pleased he had thought enough ahead to gather information he thought he might eventually need. "Four girls in fifteen years, and considering today's morals, that is a very low number."

"Those four wouldn't have happened if it hadn't been for her." Her composure began to weaken.

"They had nothing to do with Sara." His voice hardened. "Two of them got pregnant because they hadn't been told the proper facts about birth control. One because she was looking for the love and affection she couldn't get at home. The other because she wanted to marry her boyfriend and figured getting pregnant would snare him. Don't you realize most people could care less that Sara is an unwed mother? They have more important things to worry about than one person. As I said before, I wish I knew why you disliked her so much, because I think if you got to know her, you'd soon learn that she is a very lovely lady with a warm and generous personality."

Mrs. Masterson stood up. "I can see you don't care to look at the proper side to this situation, Reverend. Perhaps if you started thinking about getting married, your mind wouldn't be taken up with a woman who could do nothing but drag you down in the mud with her. I'd honestly hate to see that happen, because we have enjoyed your preaching. But..." She left the obvious unsaid.

"Yes, perhaps I should think more seriously about marriage and settling down." There was a mocking lilt to his voice, but she didn't notice it. "I also suggest you do some reading. Especially the story about the woman at the well."

Mrs. Masterson knew exactly what he was talking about. "Good night, Reverend." Her tone was as frosty as her eyes. "Think over what I've said. It would be to your best interests. Don't bother, I'll see myself out."

BY MORNING SARA HAD MADE her decision and was determined to speak with Jackson before she lost her nerve. "Jackson, I've finally decided to sell the station and the house," she announced during breakfast after Tim had left for school.

The old man looked up at her. "'Cause of the preacher?"

She nodded. "There's more going on than I can handle, so I think the best thing I can do is go away."

Jackson mumbled under his breath. "Just give me enough time to pack my stuff is all I ask."

Her face revealed surprise. "You'd come with us?"

"Hell, yes," he said gruffly. "Someone's got to watch after you. Woman, if you thought you were gonna get rid of me, you're wrong."

Sara jumped up and hugged him. "You know, I don't feel so alone now." She glanced at the clock. "Time for work. I'll make my calls from the station. Oh, let's not tell Tim just yet. He's doing well, and I don't want him upset until it's necessary."

"You better talk to that judge, too," Jackson advised.

She grimaced. "I forgot about him," she confessed. She only hoped he wouldn't create a problem she couldn't solve.

Luckily the first part of the morning kept them both busy so Sara didn't have very much time to worry about what she was going to do. As soon as things slowed she called a realtor and arranged to have the house and station listed. She was told she might not have long to wait for a sale, since there had been several people looking for a local business to invest in. With that done Sara then called Judge Carmody's office and set up an appointment to see the man the next week. It wasn't a visit she was looking forward to. When she finished her calls, she noticed Jackson watching her from the garage area and that the man's face looked sad.

"Jackson, you don't have to go," she said quietly. "After all, this town has been your home all your life. I could arrange that you be kept on at the station."

He shook his head. "No sirree, I go where you go," he said firmly. "But if I were you, I'd have a long talk with the preacher."

Sara smiled wearily. "If you were me, you'd understand why I can't do that."

JESS PARKED HIS TRUCK in front of the drugstore and nodded to several people he knew as he entered the building, which still boasted an old-fashioned soda fountain. As he perused the various brands of shave foam his ears pricked up when he heard Sara's name spoken with an air of disgust.

"I still can't believe she was brazen enough to show up at the Marcys' party. If it hadn't been for the minister, I just know Geraldine wouldn't have allowed her inside." A woman Jess silently identified as Marge Wardlow, the dentist's wife, spoke in too loud a voice. "I just wonder what she did to charm the minister into taking her. Such a nice man he is, too. If only he knew what kind of woman she really is. It just isn't right,

Sharon. Look how she's tried to seduce your own husband.''

If he hadn't felt so angry, Jess would have laughed at the woman's righteous indignation. Sharon Patterson was Albert's long-suffering wife. He remained in that one spot, not caring if anyone noticed him. He intended to hear this conversation to the end.

"There was a time when women like her were run out of town." Sharon's strident voice carried through the store. "It's disgusting. I'm surprised Cora Masterson hasn't done something by now."

"There isn't much we can do, but I do know I'll travel the extra miles to get my gas, and I'm telling my Tom he isn't to keep her as a patient," Marge went on. "I'll tell you something. We can make it very difficult for that woman to live here, and maybe she'll get the right idea and move. And as far as I'm concerned it can't be any too soon."

Jess spun on his heel. Part of him wanted to storm over to the other aisle and confront the women with their vicious tongues. He wanted nothing more than to blast them with good old-fashioned fire and brimstone, but he knew with his anger so strong at the moment he would undoubtedly say things he would later regret. He left the store without picking up what he needed. He got into his truck and roared down the street faster than usual. It wasn't until he was a good distance out of town that he slowed and eventually pulled over to the side of the road.

He sat there pounding his steering wheel again and again while damning women like Marge and Sharon who had nothing better to do than slander someone who had never done a thing to harm them. When he felt more in control, he breathed deeply to contain his temper. He wondered if all this would have happened if he hadn't arrived here? And if he left Henderson for good, sought another church, would they continue persecuting her or leave her alone? He wished he knew the answer. As he sat there thinking over the alternatives he could only come to one conclusion, and he was determined not to waste any time.

Chapter Fourteen

Sara took the afternoon off to catch up on her house-keeping chores. She was in the midst of her vacuuming, completely engrossed with her work when a tap on her shoulder sent her whirling around, her mouth open to scream.

"Hey, it's only me." Jess took hold of her shoulders. "Jackson told me you were here."

She shut off the vacuum cleaner and stood still for a moment to control her racing heartbeat. "Why didn't you call out?" she demanded. "You scared me half to death."

"I did. You must not have heard me."

Sara looked at Jess's face, noting the cold anger in his eyes even though he had a smile on his face. She immediately feared the worst. "What happened?"

"Nothing for you to worry about," he replied, turning away. "Sara, we need to have a serious talk."

"About us," she guessed, walking over to an easy chair and sitting down. What had stirred him up so?

He remained standing. "I know it hasn't been all that long, but time doesn't count where intense feelings like ours are involved." He walked over to her and hunkered down in front of the chair, taking her hands in his. "Sara, I love you a great deal, and I don't want to go through the rest of my life without you. I want to help you with Tim and be there whenever you need me. And I want to be there as your husband, not your minister."

Her mouth went dry. "Oh, Jess, do you realize what you're saying?"

He grinned. "I can imagine it's not the most romantic proposal in the world, but I was never one for hearts and flowers, I'm afraid. Besides, I was afraid if I showed up with a dozen red roses and a box of candy, you'd think I was crazy."

"Yes, I probably would question your sanity." She blinked rapidly to stem the tears. "I do love you, Jess, and being your wife would be the most wonderful thing in the world, but what about any obstacles you could run up against?"

He thought about Cora Masterson, Marge Wardlow and Sharon Patterson, and they were only a few. "I have faith," he said simply. "While there are people who will say vicious things about you, there will be even more who will support you, and I will always be there. Do you realize how many people truly like and respect you? And one loves you so much it overflows." He raised her hands to his lips. "Are you willing to take that chance?"

Sara sat there taking in each word. "So many nights I would lie awake wondering if we could have a second chance," she whispered. "I also want Tim to know you as his father, not as our minister. But it won't be easy. He still feels troubled about the world in general, and I don't know how he would take the news all at once."

"We wouldn't do it that way," he assured her. "We would get married first and tell him the rest later." He drew a deep breath. "I don't want us to waste any more time. Too much has passed by for us already."

She nodded in agreement. "Ah, when?"

"Now."

Sara's eyes widened. "Now? Jess, it isn't done that way."

"It can be if we fly to Nevada," he explained. He knew there were other reasons why he wanted them to marry quickly, reasons he would have to keep from Sara. He had a feeling that if they waited some of the so-called good ladies of the town would intervene and prey on whatever insecurities Sara might have left. He hoped if she carried his name, Cora and her group would back off.

She shook her head. "Jess, if we marry quickly people will assume the worst. You know that."

"Then we make sure our first child doesn't arrive for at least eighteen months," he quipped.

Sara's face lit up. Many times she had wished for more children, but she had refused to marry just for that one reason. "You want more children?"

"I wouldn't mind. Would you?"

"No." Sara framed his face with her hands, looked deep into his eyes and saw the love he felt for her. "I feel overflowing with that same love," she murmured. "And I want to see it grow with the years. I want us to grow old together and argue over who spoils our grandchildren the most. Yes, I want to be selfish and have it all." She smiled brightly. "I'm worried about the consequences, I won't deny that. But not as worried as I would be if I denied us."

He pulled her into his arms, holding her tightly. They kneeled on the carpet hugging each other and laughing and talking all at the same time.

"I suppose you already have this planned?" Sara finally caught her breath.

"Yes. I'm going to tell Mrs. Harris I'll be out of town for a day or so. We'll make the necessary announcements when we return," he informed her.

Sara smiled at his admission that he wasn't as sure of her as he'd like to be. "I can leave anytime you want me to," she told him.

He nodded. "I'll make the arrangements and call you. But be prepared to leave this afternoon."

"All right." She leaned forward, kissing him deeply. They were lost in each other for a while before Jess pulled away, breathing deeply.

"We've got to get this wedding on the road." He exhaled a deep breath, standing up and pulling Sara to her feet.

She looked over his shoulder and caught sight of her reflection in the mirror hanging over the mantel. "Jess, you proposed to me looking like this!" she wailed, noticing her hair was tied back in an untidy ponytail, her face was smudged with dust, and her cotton work shirt looked as if it were ready for the ragbag.

He was confused by her agitation. "You look beautiful."

"Beautiful? By all rights you should have taken one look and run screaming the other way."

He kissed her lightly on her lips. "But I didn't. Look at it this way, if I could look at you when your nose is dirty and tell you how much I love you, then it has to be true. Now, lady, get ready for your wedding. I'll call you within the hour and give you the details."

Sara watched him leave, still unable to believe this was all happening to her. She had to talk to Jackson and at the same time figure out how to keep the news from

Tim until she and Jess could sit down and talk to him together. And she felt it would work out better if they did it after they came back from Nevada. She knew either way there would be problems, but she still preferred to wait. As for the present, she knew she would have to hurry to get everything done. Knowing Jess, she wouldn't have a lot of time to prepare for the trip, and her first priority was definitely a shower.

THE HOTEL SUITE WAS MORE THAN Sara visualized, but all she was aware of was the king-size bed she and Jess lay in. She looked at her hand resting on his bare shoulder, the scrolled gold band he had slipped on her finger earlier winking in the soft lamplight and knew it matched Jess's ring. While their wedding ceremony wasn't held in a church, it was still beautiful, and they promised one another to repeat their vows in a church as soon as possible. She would have luxuriated more in the idea of being Mrs. Jess Larkin, but the feel of his hands stroking her from shoulders to hips sent all sane thoughts out of her head.

"Do you realize how beautiful you are?" he murmured, as his lips traced the nipple that peaked under his touch. He wanted nothing more than to bury himself within her, but he intended this to be a proper wedding night for them.

Sara gasped when his mouth fully covered the nipple and suckled, drawing sensations from her womb. She clutched his shoulders, feeling as if she were falling into a dark pit, but she wasn't frightened because she knew Jess was with her.

"Touch me, Sara," he ordered hoarsely, transferring his attention to her other breast, intensifying the fire racing through her body while his hands explored downward until he found her moist nest of blond curls, his fingers delving inside.

Her hands fluttered blindly over his chest and down to the taut belly and beyond. When she touched him intimately, he breathed in sharply. Eager to rediscover him physically, she continued stroking and loving him as he loved her.

"It isn't fair that your body has hardly changed while I have stretch marks and a few extra pounds to show for the years," she complained.

"If it wasn't for my regular workouts, you wouldn't have looked at me twice." Jess was finding it increasingly difficult to think with Sara touching him the way she was.

"Are you kidding? I have an idea you could be bald and have a pot belly, and I'd still look at you more than twice."

"Now that is love," he chuckled, but his amusement was short-lived.

Almost at the breaking point, Jess caught her mouth with his and thrust his tongue inside with a roughness that revealed his impatience and a gentleness that revealed his love. When he entered her, it was slow and careful, his eyes looking deeply into hers. His primitive half was pleased she hadn't been with a man for a long time. Sara's moans were music to his ears as he slowly thrust in and out. Her body arched upward to be a part of him as much as possible. Words between them were incoherent, faces flushed and lips moist and parted. Sara's eyes widened as ripples of pleasure fanned throughout her body. She looked up into Jess's eyes, dark with the same feelings she experienced.

"I thought that kind of lovemaking was for kids," he murmured, rolling over onto his side and cradling her in the warmth of his arms. He kissed the damp skin of her temple, trailing his lips down to the corner of her mouth and discovering her soft smile.

"I believe we proved them wrong." She shifted her body until her cheek rested against the damp skin of his chest. "Even though we're all getting older." She took a handful of her own hair and searched through it until she found the strand she wanted. "Look at this, I'm getting gray hair. Why I don't have more, thanks to Tim, I don't know. Pretty soon I'm going to be hunting through Clairol and L'Oreal for the best color to match mine."

"I wouldn't worry if I were you," Jess told her. "Right now we have a honeymoon to celebrate, and as we only have the room until tomorrow we should concentrate on more important things. Agreed, Mrs. Larkin?"

"Agreed."

WHEN THE TIME CAME FOR THEM to return home, they felt more than a little sad at the idea of real life intruding into their private time. Sara also felt a great deal of apprehension, worrying that a certain faction of the townspeople would not accept their marriage and Jess would suffer the consequences. As if sensing her doubts, he held her hand during the flight, and with that contact she began to feel ready for anything that came their way. She was relieved she only had to wait one day to find out what would happen.

They didn't arrive in Henderson until late afternoon. Sara thought they should part and go to their respective homes, but he wasn't having any of it.

"No. We're married now, and married people stay together," he told her, raising her hand to his lips.

By Sara's direction Jess parked the Bronco behind the house, and they crept inside without being seen. Sara knew she was foolish, the news would be out soon enough, but she wanted them to have some time just for themselves. After glancing at the clock and knowing Jackson wouldn't be back at the house for a few more hours and Tim was at his job, they retired to Sara's bedroom to make up for lost time.

Much later the glow still hadn't left their bodies as they lay under the tumbled covers, content with kisses and stroking hands.

"Mom?"

"Oh, no!" Sara sat up, clutching the sheet against her as she called out, "Tim, don't—"

Her warning came too late as he opened the door. Seeing what looked like a compromising situation, he remained in the doorway. The expression he turned on Jess was dark and threatening.

"You bastard," he spat out. "What are you trying to do, ruin her even more? Get out of there, because I want to kill you."

"Tim, no!" Sara shouted, frustrated because she couldn't get out of bed. She wished her robe wasn't in her closet.

Jess was a great deal more relaxed as he leaned over, grabbed his jeans and pulled them on.

"There's a lot we have to tell you, Tim," he said calmly, standing up. "And I don't think this is the room for us to have our discussion in."

He shook his head. "Oh, no, this isn't the time to talk. You and I've done enough of that. Either you get out now, or I'll kill you here."

Sara had never felt more frightened as she watched them leave the bedroom. As soon as she could, she grabbed her clothing and pulled it on. She ran through the house until she heard the sounds of flesh striking flesh. Crying out, she burst out the back door and found Tim pummeling Jess without his fighting back.

"Tim, you're making a mistake!" she cried, running over and grabbing his arm before he could strike Jess again.

"No, I'm not. He wants to show the world you're a whore, and you're not!" He shook her off, forcing her to stumble to the ground before he went after Jess again in a blind rage.

"Tim, you don't understand the whole story. You have to listen to me, we got married yesterday," Sara screamed, standing up ready to intervene again if need be.

"You married this guy?" he hooted, hesitating just enough for Jess to stand back, the older man watchful. "Don't you realize what you've done? All the people in town are going to laugh at you! They'll say horrible things about you. Is that what you want? Why? Just tell me why you did it." Pain radiated from his face, not the physical kind but the kind that hurt even more, because it came from the spirit.

Sara sensed his sorrow and knew he felt threatened by this new piece of news. And with this realization words spilled out she later wished hadn't been spoken. "Tim, he's your father." With the last word hanging in the air she felt the tension hit her like a brick wall.

Tim's fist froze in midair. He spun around to stare at her. It didn't take an idiot to see she was telling the truth. He turned back to look at Jess, who was using his handkerchief to stem the blood flowing from his split lip.

"Wait a minute." His body quivered as he tried to take in the truth, but didn't want to believe it. "You're saying he's . . . And that you . . ."

"We knew each other in school," she said quietly.

He sliced his hand through the air to silence her. "And you married him after what he did to you back then? Mom, he left you!"

"I told you before, I left him," Sara explained. "He didn't know about you until he arrived in town. I told you before, your father didn't know where I came from. Plus there's a great deal more to the story that we can discuss at another time when we're all a great deal calmer. His coming here was pure coincidence."

"More like divine providence," Jess murmured, unfazed when Tim swung around to glare at him.

"Why didn't you ever tell me all the truth?" he demanded of his mother. "Why did I have to find out like this?" He knew the image of seeing them in bed would stay with him for a long time.

Sara walked over to her son, placing her hand on his arm. "Tim, Jess wanted you to know everything, but I wasn't sure how to tell you, and I was afraid it wouldn't go over very well with his congregation."

He laughed harshly, shrugging off her hand. "Oh, yeah, worry more about him than me. Now I know where I stand. Maybe you should have let Judge Carmody put me in jail, then the two of you could have done anything you wanted without me around." His young face was lined with bitterness.

"Tim, I want us to be a family," Jess spoke up. "But it's going to take some work from all of us."

"Tell you what, you two just start without me," he said roughly, moving away.

"Tim!" Sara called after him as he ran down to the gas station. A moment later she heard the sound of his motorcycle starting up and roaring away.

"This wasn't the way I envisioned telling him," she murmured, leaning against Jess when he put his arms around her and held her close. "I thought we could all sit down and discuss this in a rational manner."

"I won't lie, we may have additional problems on our hands," he said quietly. "But if we work together, we can handle them."

She sighed, nuzzling her face against the curve between his shoulder and throat. "I just wish I had your faith."

"You do have it, you just haven't tried it out yet."

But Sara learned she couldn't relax. When Jackson came up from the station, he told her Tim hadn't said anything before taking off on his motorcycle. Jackson congratulated them on their marriage and fixed Jess with a steely eye.

"Your marryin' her don't mean I have to go to church from now on, does it?" he asked gruffly.

Jess chuckled. "No, Jackson, that's still left up to you, although I don't think the walls would fall down if you decided to try it out."

"I'll think about it" was his decision, then he turned to Sara. "What's for dinner?"

She couldn't help laughing as she realized life went on no matter what happened.

That night Jess didn't make love to Sara. Sensing her sorrow, he just held her and offered what comfort he could as she lay awake hopelessly waiting for her son's return. When morning came, her eyes were highlighted by violet shadows. But her weariness didn't stop her from dressing carefully for her debut as the pastor's new wife.

"Are you sure we couldn't put this off for a week?" she pleaded, as they drove over to Jess's house so he could gather up his notes for his sermon and change his clothes.

"This is not a trip to the dentist, Sara," he chided, noting her apprehension. "Besides, if we're going to live together like an old married couple, I think we should begin now, or we're going to have people believing we're living in sin," he teased lightly. "Sara, he'll come around. It was a shock to him to find out the way he did, and he's going to have to work it out his own way."

She nodded, but she didn't feel as confident as he did. While Jess changed his clothes she wandered through the house, but didn't sit down, because she couldn't make herself feel comfortable there.

"You wouldn't mind living in my house?" she asked.

"Not at all."

"We wouldn't have as much privacy," Sara warned.

He grinned and dropped a kiss on the tip of her nose. "That's what locks on bedroom doors are for."

As they walked over to the church, Sara silently ordered the butterflies in army boots marching through her stomach to cease and desist. When he seated her in the front pew, she grabbed his hand, looking more frazzled than he expected.

"They won't eat you," he assured her.

"Oh, Jess, don't you understand?" she cried. "I'm not afraid for me, I'm thinking of you. I don't want them to do anything to harm you."

Loving her all the more for her unselfish thoughts, he quickly kissed her. He had just left her when several members entered the foyer. For the next twenty minutes Sara pasted on an unconcerned smile as members filed in looking at her quizzically. When Tess saw her she mimed frantic questions her way, but Sara merely smiled at her, pleased to finally get her own back. Tess started to rise once to walk over, but one of her sons caught her attention when he began tearing the program into shreds and showering them over his sister, who was loudly complaining.

Sara's composure almost broke when Mrs. Masterson fixed her with an icy glare, but she cloaked herself with Jess's love and was able to smile back at her. The older woman's step faltered, but she quickly regained her self-possession and sat down in her regular pew.

"Good morning," Jess greeted them with a warm smile. "Shall we start with singing page one hundred and ten?"

He noticed the singing was a bit sporadic as people's necks craned watching the blond woman sitting demurely in the front pew, the pew usually reserved for the minister's family.

When Jess came to the announcements, he handled the usual ones with dispatch, and then hesitated as he looked around the large chapel.

"And now I have something very special to announce." He smiled broadly as he held his hand out toward Sara. "Sara Murdock and I were married two days ago." He remained silent as collective gasps and Tess's shocked whisper "Well, I'll be damned" flew through the room.

Mrs. Masterson rose from her seat and looked at Jess for a full minute. "You've made a grave error." She turned and walked down the aisle without looking left or right.

Jess remained at the pulpit, staring out over the rest of the congregation to see who would leave next. He counted ten more people, all friends of Mrs. Masterson, leaving before the rest settled down.

"I'm glad to see that so many of you have stayed," he said. "Because that tells me you're not judging Sara for something that was beyond her control. Now instead of giving you my usual sermon, I'm going to tell you a story." He looked around, keeping eye contact. "Sixteen years ago there was a young man who was considered pretty wild. And during this period of rebellion he met a girl. A very lovely and innocent girl." His eyes rested briefly on Sara. Her returning smile was tentative, then grew stronger under the love in his gaze.

"They fell in love and experienced something they were positive could only happen to them. But they were young and immature in many ways. The girl wanted to marry because, to her, that was the next step. Unfortunately he wasn't ready and told her in a way that wasn't very tactful. Harsh words followed and she left him."

He stared down at the pulpit, looking at the hand that was clenched into a tight fist. He took several deep breaths to relax.

"Naturally he was angry, convinced in his youthful arrogance she would return to him. He should have known better. She wanted a stable life, and he wasn't prepared to give her that. He didn't know where she was from, so he told himself there wasn't any way he could look for her. But if he had wanted to badly enough, he would have. The brash side of him wouldn't allow it, and he regretted it many times.

"As time passed he grew even angrier, and he had a temper to equal Hades." He smiled wryly. "And that temper landed him in a fight and eventually, in jail." He noticed the many shocked faces before him, but also a few understanding ones. "It was there he met the man who changed his life.

"He was the jail's visiting minister, and while the young man called him obscene names and turned his back on him, he still never gave up on that boy. It was because of him he realized he could turn his life around and do something positive with it. The minister never allowed him to look back all the time he returned to school for his degree. By then he had found a purpose and decided his ministry would be working with troubled boys. And then after a while he felt the need to work in a church...and he was led here, to Henderson." His voice strengthened with each word. "I was that young man, and to this day I am convinced I was led here to find Sara again...and to meet my son."

The silence following his announcement was deafening. Sara kept her gaze on Jess, unaware of the tears streaming down her cheeks. She didn't know when she had ever been so proud of someone as she was then.

"Now I realize some of you can't accept the fact that your pastor was human during one part of his life," Jess continued. "So if you wish me to step down, I will certainly understand. I also want to tell you that I've come to love this town, and if it's your wish, I want to continue my work here."

Leon MacIntyre, a tall, lean man who acted as the church's head deacon stood up. "Reverend, we thank you for your honesty here," he said in a slow voice. "And I think you'll understand that the deacons will meet right away to discuss this."

Jess nodded as he stepped away from the pulpit. He walked over to Sara, who immediately stood up. Other than her pale face she betrayed none of the inner agitation she felt. The couple walked slowly up the aisle to the outer doors. Sara turned to ask Jess what he felt the outcome would be when a beat-up old pickup raced through the parking lot and skidded to a stop in front of the open doors. Jackson looked out of the window of the truck.

"Sara, the hospital called," he shouted. "Tim had an accident."

She swayed and would have fallen if Jess hadn't grasped her waist. "We're on our way."

Sara was so numb with shock she was unaware of Jess pushing her into the Bronco and driving with excessive speed toward the small hospital.

"Tim Murdock," he announced to the nurse the moment they burst into the emergency room. "Where is he?"

She looked through the records and indicated a seat for them while she paged the doctor. Sara refused to sit, instead paced the room until her family doctor appeared.

"Sara." He smiled briefly. "I'm afraid Tim took a pretty nasty spill off that motorcycle of his."

She gripped Jess's hand tightly. "What happened?"

"He took a side road where a couple of kids were drag racing, and he ended up in a ditch." The doctor shook his head with disgust. "He's got some broken bones, and I'm afraid there might be some internal bleeding, and I'm going to have to go in and take a look." He squeezed Sara's hand. "He's a strong boy, Sara. I wouldn't worry too much. Pretty soon he'll be demanding a new motorcycle."

"He's not getting his license until he's thirty," she announced, her voice quivering.

"Try and take it easy. I'll send word out when we've learned something."

Sara resumed her pacing even when Jess returned to the waiting room. Jackson, Tess and Charlie soon appeared to help keep vigil, but Sara was aware of nothing other than the thirty-two steps she took each way and the slight smell of disinfectant that assaulted her nostrils. She feared if she didn't hear some news soon she would scream.

"We were wrong to marry so abruptly," she muttered. "This is all my fault. It wouldn't have happened if we hadn't run off and married the way we did. He had two shocks in a matter of seconds, and he couldn't handle them."

"Don't blame yourself," Jess scolded, grabbing her shoulders. "You know very well he liked to ride along deserted roads. It could have happened now or later, no matter what we had done."

"He's right, Sara," Tess added. "How many times had you told Tim to be careful along some of those roads? More times than you and I would care to count."

But Sara couldn't be comforted. She kept pacing the floor, lost in a sorrow of her own making until an unexpected voice intruded.

"Sara."

Positive her ears were playing tricks on her, Sara looked up and saw Mrs. Masterson standing in the doorway.

"I hope you're happy," Sara spat out. "My son could be dying, and you've always wanted me to suffer. Well, now it's happening. Is that why you're here, to gloat?"

"Sara!" Jess said sharply.

Mrs. Masterson held up her hand to silence his further words. "No, let her talk out her pain." She looked at the others. "Could we be left alone?" All four looked wary. The older woman smiled wryly. "Please don't worry, I just would like to talk to Sara in private."

That was the first time the woman had called her by name, Sara realized, but her eyes were wary, fearing the older woman would find another one of her weaknesses and pounce on them. Or had she come here to tell Jess he was fired and wanted to tell Sara it was all her fault? Sara still didn't trust her.

"Millie Kirkpatrick told me your story," she began. For once the older woman looked uncertain. "I realize I've acted your enemy over the years."

"If that was acting, you deserve an Academy Award."

Mrs. Masterson winced. "Let me explain something to you. A story that is not well known." She sat down on the couch, her spine ramrod stiff. She went on to talk about a boy she had known in school, a boy she thought she loved, but who was deemed unsuitable by her father. And while she loved the boy she didn't love him enough to go against her father and instead married someone her father approved of. Those feelings were carried all through the years, and in her way, she envied Sara for keeping to her true love in the face of pain and sometimes hate. "I guess I resented you for your courage," she said simply.

Sara stared at her, unable to believe the woman had been so candid with her. "Courage? Oh, no, I didn't have courage. If it hadn't been for my true friends, I don't know what I would have done."

Mrs. Masterson nodded. "Yes, you are very rich in friends. My so-called friends will only stay with me as long as I have what they call power. Others call me a bitter old woman and a few other names that wouldn't bear repeating." She smiled. "I think that's why I was always so cold to you, you had what I didn't. My husband was a good man, but he was also a weak one, and I always resented him for that."

Sara bowed her head as she absorbed Mrs. Masterson's words. She doubted the older woman wanted her sympathy; it wasn't her style. Her brain was already reeling so much she doubted she could take in anything else. She wondered if Mrs. Masterson ever felt lonely; she couldn't have had true friends, after all. Too many people were afraid of her.

Just as suddenly, the older woman reverted back to her old iron-willed self. "What I have told you is not for public consumption," she said stiffly.

Sara looked up and said wryly, "Of course you would immediately suspect me of taking advantage of you. Don't worry, I don't work that way."

The faintest trace of a smile touched Mrs. Masterson's lips. "I suppose you're still going to run that gas station, which isn't the proper image for a pastor's wife."

"Other than sit here and wait until I have word about my son, I don't know what I'll do."

Eyes not faded by age looked her up and down. "Yes, you do, because you will do what you feel is right and hang the rest of the town, won't you?"

"No, not hang the town, but I can't live for everyone. I realize my life will change because of my marriage to Jess, and I'm more than willing to accept that."

Mrs. Masterson thought over her words. "We'll see," was all she said. She picked up her purse and stood up. For a moment the warmth that must have been hidden deep down inside flickered outward. "I do hope your son is all right. He's always been a wild boy. Perhaps with Reverend Larkin's direction he'll finally settle down. One thing, I know my granddaughter was behind what happened. She enjoys manipulating people too much. I only hope she learns her lesson before it's too late." With that she left, walking with stately grace past the four people in the hall.

"Sara," Jess called out to her when he saw the doctor approach them. She ran over to Jess, reaching out for his strength as he put his arm around her shoulders and hugged her tightly against him.

"He's one lucky kid," the doctor told them. "He's been in recovery for a little while, but I wanted to make sure his signs remained fairly stable before I came out to see you. He's been drifting in and out for about the past twenty minutes."

"May we see him?" she begged.

He smiled. "I didn't think I'd be able to keep you away for too long."

Sara and Jess approached the bed Tim lay in. She choked back a sob as she stared at all the apparatus used to keep his vital signs monitored and the sling holding his plaster-encased leg off the bed.

"He looks so small," she breathed, holding her fingers against her lips.

Tim's eyes fluttered open. "Hi," he croaked. "My bike's pretty messed up, huh?"

"Your bike? If I were you I wouldn't worry so much about that as about you getting well," she gasped, trying hard not to cry. "You don't look so good yourself."

Tim looked past her toward Jess. "I did a lot of thinking last night before all this happened," he whispered. "I'm still not too sure how I feel about you, but you could have written me off, and you didn't, so I guess I should try to do the same."

Jess's smile was wobbly. "Fair enough."

Sara collapsed in the chair by Tim's bed, one of her hands holding Tim's, the other gripping Jess's. It wouldn't be easy, but they were a family, and who said families ever had it easy?

Epilogue

Sara dressed in a frilly cotton and lace robe and served dinner in the living room by candlelight. She and Jess had spent a majority of the past week at the hospital keeping watch over Tim even though the doctor and nurses patiently, and sometimes impatiently, assured them he was in excellent hands. This was the first evening they had spent home alone, and they vowed to concentrate on nothing else but each other.

"I told Jackson I'd shoot him if he came back before midnight," she announced, setting the plates on the coffee table.

They ate their meal talking occasionally, but never voicing the thought that was always in the back of their minds. No word had come from the deacon board yet, and Jess knew they would probably make a decision soon.

"Jess, they can't afford to lose someone as good as you," Sara said suddenly, reaching across the table for his hand.

He smiled and squeezed her hand. "Well, we have to wait and see, don't we? Don't worry, Sara, I've put our problem in more capable hands. What's meant to happen, will."

She nodded. "Well, eat up because the minute your plate is clean I intend to seduce you."

He grinned. "I could live with that." He proceeded to eat his dinner in record time. When finished he picked up his plate and Sara's which was still half covered with food, and carried them into the kitchen. "We're done."

Sara looked up at him, thinking of the fact she hadn't had a chance to eat since this morning and had looked forward to the steak. Without another thought she stood up and put her arms around his neck. Their lips had barely touched when the doorbell rang.

Jess sighed and seriously thought about ignoring it.

"It could be important," Sara said softly.

"Then they can send a telegram," he muttered, bending his head to hers just as the bell rang again. "All right, I can take a hint. I'll be right back. This visitor will not be staying long."

"Go get him," she teased.

Jess threw open the door prepared to offer the caller a suggestion they come back later when he realized Leon MacIntyre was standing in front of him.

"Reverend," the man greeted him. "I hope I'm not disturbing you. I stopped by the hospital, and they said you and your wife were home. I'm glad to hear the boy is doing all right."

"Thank you. Won't you please come in?" Jess stepped back.

Sara stood awkwardly in the middle of the living room, her face a bright pink with embarrassment. Most women weren't caught wearing their robes at seven o'clock in the evening.

"Mrs. Larkin." Leon inclined his head toward her.

"Please, sit down." She gestured toward the couch.

As soon as the older man was seated, he turned to Jess. "I think you can understand our decision has not been an easy one," he said without preamble. "Some of the board are pretty narrow-minded." Jess hung his head, positive he already knew why the head deacon had come. "But there's more of us who look beyond the surface. We're hoping you'll stay with us, Reverend," he explained. "A few of the men figure you're the perfect man to set up some kind of youth group for our town."

Sara exhaled a sigh of relief. "Thank God."

"Exactly," Jess murmured. "Leon, I would like to stay and work with the people I've come to know and respect."

Leon stood up. "Well, I won't keep you folks any longer." He looked down at Jess. "I can't guarantee you it will be easy, because some don't think you should stay, but the rest of us will be there supporting you." He nodded at Sara. "Mrs. Larkin."

When they were left alone, they couldn't hide their broad grins.

"It looks as if the official pastor of Henderson's Community Church resides here," Sara enthused.

He caught her up in his arms and spun her around. "And he's a very happy man," he laughed, then sobered. "Leon's right, it won't be easy. We'll have a lot of hard work ahead of us."

"You're a fighter, Jess," she reminded him. "You'll do fine."

He thought about the work ahead of him and knew she was right. But he also knew it could be worse. "One day at a time," he replied. "We'll just take it one day at a time and things will work out."

Sara smiled, having been witness to the slow but steady progress he had already made with Tim. "I have no doubt about that."

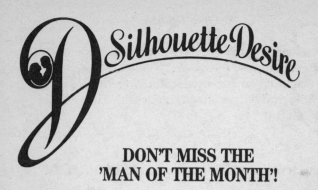

Silhouette Desire

DON'T MISS THE
'MAN OF THE MONTH'!

What makes a romance? A special man, of course, and from June to May 1990 Silhouette Desire celebrates that fact with *twelve* of them! Throughout the year there are a dozen novels with a tribute to the Silhouette Desire hero — our **MAN OF THE MONTH!**

Sexy, rugged, charming, irritating ... irresistible! Nothing can stop these men from sweeping you away.

Written by some of your favourite authors, each man is custom-made for reading pleasure — so don't miss a single one.

June — Blake Donavan in RELUCTANT FATHER by Diana Palmer
July — Hank Branson in THE GENTLEMAN INSISTS by Joan Hohl
August — Carson Tanner in NIGHT OF THE HUNTER by Jennifer Greene
September — Slater McCall in A DANGEROUS KIND OF MAN by Naomi Horton
October — Luke Harmon in VENGEANCE IS MINE by Lucy Gordon
November — Quinn McNamara in IRRESISTIBLE by Annette Broadrick

And that's only the half of it —
So don't miss the chance to find your dream hero!

Available from Boots, Martins, John Menzies, W.H. Smith, Woolworths and other paperback stockists.

Silhouette Sensation

A marvellous new series from Silhouette!

JUNE TITLES

SUMMER OF THE WOLF
Patricia Gardner Evans

TEARS OF THE RENEGADE
Linda Howard

THE DUCK SHACK AGREEMENT
Muriel Jensen

WE GIVE THANKS
Linda Randall Wisdom